THE
PESKI
KIDS

Books by R. A. Spratt

The Adventures of Nanny Piggins
Nanny Piggins and the Wicked Plan
Nanny Piggins and the Runaway Lion
Nanny Piggins and the Accidental Blast-Off
Nanny Piggins and the Rival Ringmaster
Nanny Piggins and the Pursuit of Justice
Nanny Piggins and the Daring Rescue
Nanny Piggins and the Race to Power
The Nanny Piggins Guide to Conquering Christmas

Friday Barnes: Girl Detective
Friday Barnes: Under Suspicion
Friday Barnes: Big Trouble
Friday Barnes: No Rules
Friday Barnes: The Plot Thickens
Friday Barnes: Danger Ahead
Friday Barnes: Bitter Enemies
Friday Barnes: Never Fear

The Peski Kids: The Mystery of the Squashed Cockroach

THE PESKI KIDS

THE MYSTERY OF THE SQUASHED COCKROACH

R. A. Spratt

PUFFIN BOOKS

PUFFIN BOOKS
UK | USA | Canada | Ireland | Australia
India | New Zealand | South Africa | China

Penguin Books is part of the Penguin Random House group of companies
whose addresses can be found at global.penguinrandomhouse.com.

First published by Penguin Random House Australia Pty Ltd, 2018

Cover design by Tasha Dixon
Illustrations by Erica Salcedo
Internal design and typesetting by Midland Typesetters, Australia
Printed in Australia by Griffin Press, an accredited ISO AS/NZS 14001:2004
Environmental Management Systems printer

A catalogue record for this
book is available from the
National Library of Australia

ISBN: 978 0 14378 881 2

penguin.com.au

To Violet and Samantha

PROLOGUE

The line shuffled forward. Dr Banfield had just checked in for her flight. She was hoping to get back before the children came home from school. She only needed to pass through security, then she would be able to sit down and relax in the lounge, as much as you can relax surrounded by a thousand sweaty, nervous strangers. But the line was taking forever.

There was a family in front of her fussing over their hand luggage. They seemed to have broken every airport security rule – liquids, scissors, bottle openers. They had everything they shouldn't in their bags.

Finally, their things passed through the X-ray machine for the last time and Dr Banfield was able to lift her one carry-on suitcase onto the conveyor. She rifled through the pockets of her old tweed jacket, digging out her spare glasses, throat lozenges and tissues. She dropped them into a plastic tray, then stepped through the metal detector.

Security guards never wanted to pat her down or do an explosive test on her bag. She was a frumpy middle-aged lady. She was harmless. They barely even noticed her. That was, until now. The conveyor belt juddered to a halt. Dr Banfield looked up as a man in a cheap grey suit stepped into the security area. He whispered something to the X-ray operator, then pulled Dr Banfield's suitcase aside.

He motioned for Dr Banfield to join him at the counter. This had never happened to her before. She watched as the man in the suit opened her suitcase and searched through her dirty clothes and museum paperwork.

'What's this?' asked the man, with a thick accent. He pulled something out from the bottom of the suitcase. It was a large bone.

'The ulna of a stegosaurus,' said Dr Banfield. 'It was found in Kiev. It is particularly significant because the striations on the bone appear to be the teeth marks of a sabre-toothed tiger, which would be the earliest known confirmation of that species on the Asian continent.'

'Really?' said the man in the suit. 'We'll see about that.' He raised the bone and whacked it down hard on the edge of the counter.

'No!' cried Dr Banfield. 'It's a crucial fossil for understanding the evolution of mammals in Eastern Europe.'

The man in the suit apparently did not like being yelled at by a frumpy middle-aged lady. He looked angry now as he raised the bone again and smashed it down even harder. It shattered into a thousand fragments, but lying in the middle was something black and shiny. A small USB drive.

The man in the suit picked it up. 'What do we have here?'

'I've got no idea how that got there,' said Dr Banfield. She turned pale. Her eyes gaped wide. This was going terribly wrong.

'You'd better come with me,' said the man ominously.

'But my flight?' said Dr Banfield. 'I have to get home. My children are expecting me.'

'I'm sure it will only take a few moments to clear this up,' said the man with a smile.

He was lying. It took Dr Banfield's very large brain just a millisecond to recognise this fact, another millisecond to see that two armed guards were approaching to assist him and a third millisecond to decide that her best course of action was to punch this man, in his cheap grey suit, in the throat with her wedding ring.

Dr Banfield lashed out with lightning speed, hitting the man so hard his brain was momentarily starved of oxygen and he collapsed. The two armed guards hesitated. Their smaller brains were struggling to assimilate the fact that a dowdy middle-aged lady had just felled their department head. One of them belatedly reached for his gun, but his hand had only touched the grip when Dr Banfield broke both the bones in his forearm with a brutal turning kick. She then kicked him in the knee with her other foot to knock him down too.

The other guard lunged for her. Dr Banfield ducked, slammed her elbow into his solar plexus, delivered an uppercut to his jaw and took off running.

She vaulted over the X-ray machine and sprinted back out into the check-in lobby. It would take a few seconds for reinforcements to arrive. She had to get out of there. Unfortunately, 2 pm at any airport is a busy time. People were moving slowly, dragging unwieldy luggage behind them.

Dr Banfield ran, picking up speed as she hurdled bags, bounced off passengers and dodged around trolleys, until suddenly she slammed into a brick wall. At least, that's what it felt like. She soon worked out from the grey polyester jacket pressed into her face that she had been crash-tackled. She was hoisted to her feet. The man in the suit was holding her tightly by the upper arm. He looked dishevelled.

'Dr Banfield, you are under arrest,' spat the man.

'But I'm just an academic,' said Dr Banfield, with bumbling innocence. 'A scientist. I study dinosaur bones.'

'Don't give me that,' said the man. 'You are a spy.'

Chapter 1

A BAD START

'**S**hut your face or I'll shut it for you,' said April angrily. She was a wiry girl who, like a hummingbird, had the strange ability to be in constant motion and appear eerily still at the same time.

'You can't shut a face,' said Fin, in his pedantic monotone. 'A face isn't something that opens and closes. You could ask me to shut my eyes or my mouth, but my ears and my nose are unblockable orifices.'

'I'll block them for you,' said April, 'when I punch you and they swell shut.'

Fin narrowed his eyes slightly, which was about as expressive as his features got. He was not terribly in touch with his own emotions, so they rarely affected the shape of his face.

'N-no violence,' said Joe, their older brother. He stammered when he was nervous and talking made him nervous, so he stammered quite a lot. Joe knew exactly what he wanted to say, but just as the words were about to leave his mouth they would perform some sort of acrobatics on the tip of his tongue and refuse to emerge. So generally he said very little, except for constantly reminding April and Fin not to hurt each other.

April made a scoffing noise. Their mum didn't often notice what was going on so it was pretty easy to keep things from her, like kidney-punching your brother during dessert.

April made do with shoving Fin out of the way and stomping up the front path so she got to the door first. She punched in the code. They lived in a normal suburban house, but their mother was forgetful and often lost her keys, so they'd had a pin-pad lock installed. There is a limit to how many times you can get locked out of your own home and it still feels fun. That limit is one. Having to eat raw vegetables from the garden while you wait for a locksmith is never a barrel of laughs.

As soon as they pushed into the house a whirlwind of fur leapt at April, trying to lick her face but falling short and scrabbling all over her knees instead.

'Ooh, I missed you too, Pumpkin,' gushed April, bending over to greet her beloved dog. 'I hate it when we do javelin in PE and you have to stay home.'

Pumpkin's head snapped round as Fin entered the house. The dog leapt forward and bit him on the ankle.

'Ow!' cried Fin.

'Good boy,' said April, fishing a treat out of her pocket and rewarding her dog.

'You can't train Pumpkin to bite me,' said Fin.

'I didn't train him,' protested April. 'He's just following his natural canine instincts. He can smell loser.'

Joe was a tall, and growing taller, sixteen-year-old boy. He seemed to have more muscles popping up every month, so he spent a great deal of time eating food. He left April and Fin to their argument and went into the kitchen to find a snack. He didn't have much luck. The fridge was empty. There was low-fat yoghurt and kale juice in there, but Joe didn't consider them to be food.

'Mum!' yelled Joe. But there was no reply. Joe assumed Mum was looking at a particularly engrossing dinosaur bone. He opened the pantry and sighed. There wasn't much there either, except for a half-empty jar of olives. That would see him through until dinner. He opened the jar and wandered back to the living room.

'Mum!' yelled April. 'Fin called me an idiot!'

'No,' said Fin. 'I called you an idiot savant. In that context the word "idiot" is just an adjective. "Savant" is actually a compliment. It means "to be unnaturally good at something".'

'You said she was good at something?' asked Joe. This was unusual. Fin was thirteen and April was twelve. They were, in fact, only eleven months apart. So for one month of the year they were technically the same age. And in all their lives since they had learned to speak, Fin and April had never said anything nice to each other. Not once.

'He said I was an "idiot savant",' explained April, 'at being a pain in the neck.'

'It's true,' said Fin. 'It is your one freakish talent.'

'Mum!' bellowed April again. Their mother didn't have many rules, and the few rules she did have were rarely enforced. But she was adamant that they should not call each other 'idiot' or 'stupid', so April knew if she presented her argument well, she might get Fin in trouble.

'If you dob me in,' said Fin, 'I'll tell her what you did at lunchtime.'

'I didn't do anything at lunchtime,' said April.

'You wrestled Michael Harrigan to the ground,' said Fin.

Now April rolled her eyes. 'He loved it,' she said, tucking her wavy dark hair behind her ear.

'You d-did promise not to wrestle anymore,' Joe reminded her.

'The headmaster made you sign a contract saying you wouldn't,' Fin added.

'I didn't hurt Michael,' said April.

'You tore his shirt,' said Fin, with his characteristic irritating accuracy.

'He should learn to sew,' April retorted. 'It's an important life skill.'

'Fine,' said Fin. 'Then you won't mind me telling Mum about it. Mum!'

'You are the worst!' said April, clenching her fists. If she was about to get in trouble for wrestling, she might as well do some more wrestling to make it worthwhile.

'Where is she?' said Joe, looking at the ceiling.

Their mother did not live in the ceiling. She had an office directly above the kitchen. Normally if they yelled and screamed long enough, they would hear their mother's chair slide back as she got up and started down the stairs so she could shout at them to be quiet. But there were no sounds from above.

'Did she say she was staying late at the museum?' asked Joe.

Their mother was a palaeontologist. A very senior and well-respected one. But the thing about spending all day with a bunch of bones that are three hundred million years old is that nothing is ever really urgent. If it's waited three hundred million years, it can wait another day. So their mother was very rarely late home, unless she accidentally got stuck in a lift or forgot her pass to get out of the car park. Which she did with surprising regularity. If you can't keep track of your own house key, remembering a pass card is going to be pretty difficult too.

'Maybe she got lost again,' said April.

Their mother often got lost, particularly in shopping centres and shopping centre car parks. But she would usually just get a taxi home, pick up the kids and get them to help her find the car.

Joe looked at the answering machine next to the telephone. The light wasn't flashing. There were no messages. She would have left a message if she was delayed.

'She's probably fallen asleep,' said Fin. He went over to the staircase and bounded up the stairs two at a time. 'It was pancakes for breakfast. That always makes her sleepy.'

They heard Fin throw open the office door.

'Mum?' he called, but there was no answer. Joe and April heard Fin looking in the other rooms upstairs. 'She's not here.'

'I'll check the shed,' said Joe, trudging towards the back door.

'Why? Do you think she decided to mow the lawn?' asked April sarcastically. Their mother had never mowed the lawn. She didn't understand the western cultural obsession with short grass. Some of their more zealous neighbours had pleaded with her to let them do it, saying that long grass encouraged snakes. But their mother said she liked snakes. A very low percentage of them were venomous, and they lived 2.3 kilometres from the nearest hospital. So even if one of them was bitten by a venomous snake, they would easily be able to access antivenom in time.

It only took Joe a few seconds to cross their small yard to the tiny shed where their mother kept things she didn't use very often, like the vacuum cleaner and the ironing board. Mum wasn't there. Joe came back, shaking his head. 'Where could she b-b-be?'

Even April was starting to get concerned and generally she didn't stop being angry long enough to be concerned about anything other than herself.

Pumpkin ran to the front door and started barking.

Fin jogged back down the stairs. 'What's he barking about now?'

'The struggles of indigenous people in Papua New Guinea,' said April.

Fin looked at her, confused.

'As if we know why he's barking!' snapped April. 'I don't have dog ESP.'

'True, how can you have Extra-Sensory Perception when you barely have regular perception,' agreed Fin.

That was the straw that broke the camel's back. April launched herself at Fin, grabbing him by the collar and wrenching him sideways to pull him off his feet. But twelve years of living with April had taught Fin a thing or two about self-defence tactics. He grabbed April's wrists and dropped his weight on them so as he fell he brought her down too. April was just about to put Fin in a headlock and start administering noogies when there was an almighty BANG!

Their front door exploded inwards. Splintered wood flew everywhere and a stocky, black-clad figure wearing a full face mask burst into the room. The children found themselves looking down the barrel of a handgun.

'Oh, it's you,' said the gunwoman, in an unexpectedly familiar feminine voice. She holstered the gun and pulled off her face mask.

'Professor M-M-Maynard?' exclaimed Joe. 'Is that you?'

Now I must pause to explain a few things. Joe recognised this gunwoman because Professor Maynard was their mother's boss. Joe, Fin and April's mother was a very dowdy middle-aged woman. She wore frumpy, practical clothes, cheap thick-framed glasses and often forgot to brush her hair for several weeks at a time. So to them, their mother's boss was frumpiness squared. She was just like their mother only more so, and older. She was the type of woman you'd expect to absentmindedly offer you the used tissue she'd pulled out of her sleeve cuff, not the type of woman you'd expect to burst into your home dressed like a ninja and brandishing a weapon.

'Yes, I'm afraid it is me,' said Professor Maynard. 'Terribly sorry about that. It can't be much fun for you to have an old lady waving a taser at you when you should be doing your homework.'

'That's a taser?' asked Fin. 'It looks a lot like a real gun.'

'Don't be a silly sausage,' said Professor Maynard. 'It would totally be against the rules to point a gun at children. But they make our tasers look like guns so they're more terrifying.' She got the taser out again. 'See for yourself.' Professor Maynard pulled the trigger and blasted the potted aspidistra that sat in the corner of the living room. The plant hissed and juddered as several thousand volts of electricity flooded through it.

'I think I'd rather get shot,' said Fin, as the leaves of the plant turned brown, then black and then started to singe.

'Whoops, sorry,' said Professor Maynard, releasing the trigger. 'I'm sure with a bit of water it'll perk up again.' The plant was now slumped and dripping brown green gloop. 'Never mind about that,' said Professor Maynard, stepping in front of the plant so the children would stop looking at it. 'I expect you're surprised to see me.'

This was an understatement. Professor Maynard had only been to their house twice before. Once when their mother had locked herself out, and another time when their mother forgot to come back from a conference in Uzbekistan and Professor Maynard had popped over until they could arrange a babysitter.

'I'm here to give you some very good news,' said Professor Maynard. She smiled happily to emphasise how good the news was and how lucky they were to be about to hear it. 'Your mother is in jail in a secret prison somewhere in Eastern Europe and will probably be there for a very long time.'

The children were horrified.

'How is that good news?' asked April.

'Because she's not dead,' said Professor Maynard. 'We're all very relieved she's not dead. The Kolektiv can be a little trigger happy, so she dodged a bullet there. Literally, in fact!' Professor Maynard laughed at her own joke. Although, to the children, it did not seem terribly funny.

'Why is she in jail?' asked Fin. 'She's a palaeontologist. Did she do something wrong to a woolly mammoth bone or something?'

'W-W-What's she even doing in E-E-Eastern Europe?' asked Joe.

'She didn't say anything about leaving the country at breakfast this morning,' added Fin.

'Yes, well, she's not allowed to tell you things like that,' said Professor Maynard. 'You don't have clearance.'

'What?' said April. She was finding this conversation very confusing and upsetting, and when April was confused or upset it was usually only a short time before she started wrestling.

'I have been authorised to give you some basic details,' said Professor Maynard. 'But it's very important for your own safety that you don't know too much. So I'm going to tell you something and you're going to have lots of questions, but please don't ask them because I won't be able to answer.'

The children just stared at her. Now they were all confused.

'Your mother is not a palaeontologist,' said Professor Maynard. 'Well, technically she is. She's fully qualified and her PhD is genuine, but that's only a cover. She did her doctorate thesis over a rainy weekend to give herself a nice credible backstory.'

'Then what is she?' asked Joe.

'An international super spy,' said Professor Maynard.

'What?!' yelled all three children in unison.

'Yes, it is surprising, isn't it?' agreed Professor Maynard. 'That's why she really is such a top agent. She's just so good at convincing people she is a dowdy middle-aged academic, that it's no trouble at all for her to slip into another country and bump off a head of state.'

'She assassinates heads of state?!' said Fin.

'No, of course not,' said Professor Maynard. 'Forget I said that. And I mean that. Forget it, because if you don't, I have access to equipment that will make you forget it.'

'Okay,' said Fin, starting to edge away.

'Now, I don't want you to worry,' said Professor Maynard. 'We are doing everything in our power to get your mother out. We're looking at the satellites, diverting submarines and planning a precision missile launch any day now. But in the meantime, I'm afraid I'm going to have to ask you to pack a bag and come along with me.'

'W-W-What?' asked Joe. He was speaking for Fin and April here as well. This accurately summarised their sentiments.

Professor Maynard wagged her finger at Joe and chuckled. 'Uh-uh, no follow-up questions, remember? And I must urge you to hurry.' She glanced at her watch. 'There is a Kolektiv hit team on its way here right now. They should be arriving in about ninety seconds. So if you could pack a few things in the next seventy seconds or so, that should give us enough time to run out to the car and get away before they start firing.'

The children wasted the next five seconds just staring at the crazy lady who had burst into their house.

Professor Maynard shook her head sadly. 'I knew there would be follow-up questions. There always are.

Don't worry, I understand. You're children. You're in shock. I'll have my people handle it.' Professor Maynard brought her wrist to her mouth and barked into her cuff. 'Alpha team! Go, go, go!'

There was a one-second pause, then twelve burly, black-clad men burst into the house. Three of them grabbed the children. Another grabbed Pumpkin. They heard the man scream in pain as Pumpkin bit him. The others streamed upstairs. The children were bustled outside into a black mini-van parked by the kerb. The other men were now streaming back out of the house, carrying the family's assortment of suitcases with loose socks and undies half-hanging out of their hastily shut lids. 'House is clear!' barked the last man out.

'Good work,' said Professor Maynard. 'But we'll have to do some spring cleaning before the Kolektiv boys arrive.' The driver passed Professor Maynard what looked like a can of whipped cream. She ripped off the lid with her teeth and tossed it through the open front door of the house.

'Fire in the hole!' yelled Professor Maynard. The men took cover and Joe, Fin and April watched as their normal suburban home exploded in a ball of fire.

'Hit it, Eric!' Professor Maynard told the driver, and the mini-van squealed away. April and Fin whipped around. Through the back window, they caught a glimpse of a black BMW turn into the street just as the mini-van disappeared around the corner.

Chapter 2

WHAT'S IN A NAME?

'**Y**ou just blew up our house!' wailed Fin.

'Correct,' said Professor Maynard, turning to smile at the three children on the back seat. 'Although technically the house belonged to the agency, so I was just blowing up our own property.'

'But the stuff inside the house was ours,' said April. You could tell she was in shock. Partly because she was shaking and her lips were starting to turn blue, but also because she hadn't attacked Professor Maynard yet, which would have been her normal reaction to someone destroying all but a suitcase worth of her things.

'I know,' said Professor Maynard, in the tone of voice of someone trying to be kind when they're not naturally good at it. 'But you have to try to focus on the positive side. You're not dead.'

'You have a very l-l-low benchmark for p-positive,' stammered Joe. He was in shock too. Being a teenage boy, Joe was terrible at dealing with emotions. There is something about hormones that makes emotions go crazy for most young people between the ages of fourteen and nineteen. He wasn't sure what to be the most upset about, the fact that his mother was in a foreign prison or the fact that the olives he had been about to eat were now a smouldering pile of ash.

'Where are you taking us?' asked Fin.

'Not the prison where they're holding Mum?' asked April.

'Heavens, no,' chuckled Professor Maynard. 'I'm taking you to your father's house.'

'What?!' exclaimed all three children.

'Your dad,' said Professor Maynard, just in case the three children didn't know what the word 'father' meant. That would be odd, because two out of three of them had done incredibly well on the IQ test the agency had secretly performed on them by posing as student teachers and infiltrating their preschool. Only April hadn't because at the age of four she had refused to do the test, saying tests were patriarchal.

'But why would we visit *him*?' asked Fin.

'We haven't seen him in years,' said Joe.

'We've never seen him,' said April, indicating herself and Fin. Their father had left shortly after her birth, a fact that may go a long way towards explaining April's hostility to male authority figures.

'We don't want to go and stay with that deadbeat!' said Fin, starting to get angry. When your house has just been blown up, it's easy to get worked up quickly. 'He's never wanted anything to do with us. He's always been too busy winning the Chelsea flower show and travelling the world searching for new and exotic plants. We don't want anything to do with him.'

'Besides, isn't he in P-Papua New Guinea?' said Joe. 'Collecting samples of some r-rare carnivorous orchid?'

'I thought it was a dahlia,' said April.

'Mum told me it was a tree fern,' said Fin.

24

'Yes, your mum is very convincing, isn't she,' said Professor Maynard proudly. 'She always performs off the charts in her lying tests.'

'You test lying?' asked April.

'Oh yes, it's an essential skill for a secret agent to be able to lie up hill and down dale.' She chuckled again. 'She once lied her way into Tehran's secret service headquarters by telling the guard she had dropped a contact lens in the bathroom. He spent quarter of an hour on his hands and knees helping her look for it. All the while, she was downloading data from their mainframe using a scanner she had hidden in her handbag.' Professor Maynard sighed happily at the memory. 'She doesn't even wear contacts.'

'So where is Dad?' asked Joe. He was the only one who had any lingering regard for their father, because he was the only one who could remember him.

'In hiding,' said Professor Maynard. 'For the first eight years of their marriage your father was entirely convinced that your mother really was a dedicated palaeontologist. He was as happily married as any man who would secretly prefer to sit around in his underwear can be.'

'Then what happened?' asked April.

'He went out to dinner with your mother,' said Professor Maynard. 'It was a big deal for them. With three young children, they rarely ate out. Regrettably, a terrorist from Interpol's top ten most wanted list sat down at the next table. Obviously, your mother was duty bound to follow the reprobate to the bathroom, choke him with his own neck tie and call in a military helicopter to extract him from the roof of the building.'

'And Dad saw the whole thing?' asked Fin.

'No, actually,' said Professor Maynard. 'Your father is such a passionately dedicated horticulturalist that his ability to not notice things is off the charts.'

'You secretly tested that too, didn't you?' asked April.

'Oh yes,' said Professor Maynard. 'It's probably why he and your mother had such a happy marriage. He never noticed anything she was up to. The only problem on this occasion was that the restaurant served particularly delicious iced tea. Your father had drunk three glasses of it and, having a healthy urinary system, he needed to use the rest room at precisely the same moment your mother was dragging the terrorist up the stairs by his feet.'

'What did Dad do?' asked Joe.

'He started to hyperventilate,' said Professor Maynard, 'which was probably for the best because he passed out, giving your mother time to get the terrorist into the waiting helicopter. But just as she was coming down the stairs to get your father out of the restaurant, the other members of the terrorist cell arrived.'

'Oh dear,' said Fin.

'Precisely,' said Professor Maynard. 'Your mother is excellent at knife fighting, so she was never in any real danger, but I think the brutal way in which she broke the noses, collarbones and kneecaps of her assailants scared the living daylights out of your dad. One of the terrorists got away before your mother could subdue him and your father's identity was compromised.'

'What does that mean?' asked Joe.

'We had to hide your dad, for his own good,' said Professor Maynard. 'He was scared of your mother too.' She turned to Fin. 'You know how you totally freak out about spiders?'

'How do you know I hate spiders?' asked Fin.

'Oh, we know everything about you,' laughed Professor Maynard. 'You'd be amazed at the nooks and crannies we've stuck secret cameras in just so we can keep an eye on you. Anyhoo, the way you feel about a big hairy spider is the same way your father feels about your mother.'

'He screams and tries to run away?' asked Joe.

'Pretty much,' said Professor Maynard. 'But usually his legs go to jelly so he doesn't get far.'

'So you're sending us to stay with him?' asked April incredulously.

'That's right,' said Professor Maynard. 'It's the safest place for you. Now that your identities have been compromised.'

'What do you mean our identities have been compromised?' asked Joe.

'We don't know what your mother has been forced to tell the Kolektiv,' said Professor Maynard.

'You just said she was off the charts at lying,' said Fin.

'Yes, but they know that too,' said Professor Maynard. 'They figured out her identity from her cover ID. That's how they found out about your house. It's only a matter of time before they discover she has three children, and they'll want to get hold of you to use as leverage against her.'

'What's Mum been doing?' asked April.

'You don't want to know,' said Professor Maynard. 'I wish I didn't know. And it's my job to know everything.'

'I'm f-finding this hard to f-follow,' said Joe.

'Don't worry,' said Professor Maynard. 'It's pretty simple really. You're going to go and live with your dad. He lives in a lovely country town called Currawong.'

'You're kidding me,' said Fin. 'That's the name of a place?'

'It's a delightful town,' said Professor Maynard. 'We've enrolled you in the local school. It will be splendid. Like a holiday! The only thing is, you've got to totally forget your surname was ever Banfield. You're getting a new name.'

'What's it going to be now?' asked Fin.

'Peski,' said Professor Maynard.

'Yes, I'm sure it is irritating,' said April. 'But what's our new name?'

'No, Peski is your new name,' said Professor Maynard. 'P-E-S-K-I with an "I" you see, not a "Y". It was actually your father's maiden name before he got married. His family changed it from Peshcynski after they emigrated from Poland when he was a baby.'

'Wait,' said Joe. 'How can he have a maiden name? I thought women had maiden names.'

'That's not very progressive of you, is it?' said Professor Maynard. 'Why should it always be the woman who changes her name when she gets married?'

'Because it is,' said Fin.

'Yes, well, in this case your father agreed to change his name to your mother's name,' said Professor Maynard. 'Although, of course, Banfield isn't really her name either.' Professor Maynard laughed at the irony of this.

'It's not?' said April. This, more than anything that had happened in the last twenty minutes, made her want to punch something. It was one thing to have to change your name for security reasons, but it was another to find out your name had always been made up for security reasons.

'Oh yes, she just came up with that one off the top of her head,' said Professor Maynard, reminiscing. 'Probably because she was putting on a bandaid while looking at a field at the time.'

'So we've got to start our lives over in a new house, at a new school, with a dad we don't know and our name is going to be "Peski",' said April. 'You do realise that everyone at school is going to tease us, calling us "The Peski Kids".'

'Don't worry,' said Professor Maynard. 'The Kolektiv is after you now. Having a silly name is the least of your troubles.'

Chapter 3

DAD

Wherever Currawong was, it was a long car ride. Fin had asked why they couldn't take a helicopter and Professor Maynard had characteristically just laughed. She said helicopters were only for fictional spies like James Bond. Real spies had to use quieter means of transport. They drove all afternoon and into the night. The mini-van had snacks, but they were health food bars and fruit, so while the children didn't starve, they weren't happy.

Eventually they all found the least uncomfortable positions in their seats and drifted off to sleep, lulled by the sound of the engine and Pumpkin's gentle snores. If during the long night the van did bump over anything and jolt them awake, there was nothing to see. It was pitch black outside. There were no street lights. All they could see was the long country road stretching out ahead of them as far as the glow of the headlights could show. They soon drifted back to sleep again.

———

'Wakey, wakey!'

The children were awoken by the irritating cheerfulness of Professor Maynard. They grumbled and groaned as they stretched and sat upright. It was early morning. Looking out the window they could see they were bumping along a long dirt driveway, a line of trees either side.

'Where are we?' asked Joe.

'Home!' said Professor Maynard.

Fin sniffed. He didn't want to cry. But he had just remembered that their real home had been blown up yesterday and that their mother was in prison at an undisclosed location. Admittedly, she had never been the most motherly of mothers, and now it turned out she had been lying to them all their lives because she was a super dangerous spy, but she had always been cheerful and available for hugs. Fin would have quite liked a hug at that moment.

'Dad lives here?' said April, peering out at the beautiful rolling lawn and tall deciduous trees drooping with a thick canopy of impossibly green leaves.

'He does indeed,' said Professor Maynard.

'All these years I've imagined him living in a treehouse in Papua New Guinea,' said April.

'I'm sure he could build you a treehouse,' said Professor Maynard. 'He's certainly got lots of trees and he's good at tinkering with things.'

The van bumped around a bend in the driveway and up ahead they could see a house. It was an old ramshackle farmhouse with two storeys and a verandah wrapped all the way around the outside. It desperately needed repainting. There was an odd assortment of junk abandoned everywhere and the corrugated iron roof looked alarmingly rusty. But even with all those faults, it looked somehow elegant. A tired and genteel home surrounded by so much abundantly healthy vegetation. In contrast to the abandoned, rusty machinery of indeterminate purpose, the flower-beds were overflowing with beautiful arrangements of decorative plants. Bees and butterflies darted in and out of the exotic flowers.

'Is he glad we're c-coming?' asked Joe. At sixteen, he was used to adults letting him down. But he still felt nervous, hoping that it wouldn't happen.

'I'm sure he *will* be,' said Professor Maynard.

'You haven't told him we're coming, have you?' asked Fin.

'Oh no,' said Professor Maynard. 'Your father is a wonderful, kind-hearted fellow, but you don't know him as well as I do. I'm sure he will be delighted to see *you*. He is, however, the teensiest bit terrified of *me*. If he knew I was coming, he might have made a run for it.'

The van pulled up in front of the house and the children got out. Pumpkin bounded forward to pee on a lovely display of flowering daphne. Professor Maynard strode straight up to the front door, the children following her at a cautious distance. The Professor rapped loudly with the knocker.

'Is that a methane generator?' asked Fin, looking at an unusually shaped piece of machinery sitting by the front door.

'Probably,' said Professor Maynard, giving it a quick glance. 'Your dad does love his little toys.' Professor Maynard rapped on the door again.

Suddenly they heard a loud clatter, a thud, scuffling noises and the sound of someone pleading to be 'let go'. Pumpkin started barking excitedly, sensing violence in the air. But April picked him up. She wanted a hug and she was much more comfortable clutching her dog than a person.

'Ah, that'll be him,' said Professor Maynard, walking along the verandah to see down the side of the house.

Eric, the driver, had a man in a painful-looking wristlock and was half-dragging him around to the front of the house. As Eric and his captive drew closer, the children got their first look at their father in eleven years. It was disappointing.

For a start, their dad was eleven years older than they remembered him being. He had a long, badly trimmed beard, wild uncombed hair and the sort of screwed-up, wrinkly face you only get if you worry a lot and never use moisturiser. The children could have forgiven most of this because they weren't expecting him to be handsome but, being teenagers, they were acutely conscious of when an adult is embarrassing. And in this, the first glimpse of their father in so many years, he was wearing a long scruffy dressing-gown that clearly showed his naked ankles and hairy calves. It was not a dignified look.

'Harold!' cried Professor Maynard, completely ignoring the fact that her driver still had him in a wristlock. 'So wonderful to see you. You're looking well.'

'What do you want with me?' moaned their father. 'Please don't say I have to be brave. I just haven't got it in me.'

'Nothing of the kind,' said Professor Maynard. 'I've got a marvellous surprise for you. I've brought you your children! All you have to do is parent them.'

Dad peered at Professor Maynard. He didn't have his glasses on, but now he looked closer he noticed three indistinct shapes on the verandah near her. He used his free hand to reach into his dressing-gown pocket, retrieve his glasses and awkwardly put them on his face.

He wouldn't have described them as children. Three sullen teenagers were glaring warily back at him.

'A girl and two boys,' said Dad. 'I do have a girl and two boys. Are these them?' He was whispering.

37

He spent so much time dealing with plants that he was used to whispering to himself.

'Yes, that's right,' said Professor Maynard. 'I'm glad you've caught up so quickly. I'm afraid Bertha's got herself in a spot of bother over in Kolektiv-controlled territory, so you are going to have to step up and look after them.'

'They're to live with me?' asked Dad in wonder. His face drained of all colour.

Fin sniffed and stuck his bottom lip out.

Joe started mentally running through all the things he would have to do if Dad refused to look after them and he had to be in charge. He'd have to drop out of school, get a job, rent a house . . .

'Have you got a problem with that?' asked April, a hint of menace in her voice. She was already angry with her mother for secretly being incredibly exciting behind her back, and she was quite ready to take her anger out on the one parent who was actually there.

'No,' said Dad, shaking his head so his beard quivered. 'It's . . . wonderful!' Then he burst into tears.

Joe, Fin and April glanced at each other. They had never known a grown-up to cry so easily. Their mother was never weepy, although in hindsight this may have been because she was a ruthless international operative.

'Eric, be a dear,' said Professor Maynard. 'Go and make Mr Peski a nice cup of tea.'

Eric hurried off to perform this task with the same urgency with which he had passed Professor Maynard the bomb that had blown up the children's house just the previous day.

———

Half an hour later, after several cups of tea, Dad was still struggling to get a hold of himself. Professor Maynard had explained the situation numerous times, and patted him bracingly on the back so often that his shoulder was beginning to bruise.

Eric had carried the children's suitcases in and Joe, Fin and April had hurried upstairs to argue over who was going to get the best bedroom.

It turned out to be a surprisingly short argument. They usually devoted a lot of energy into arguing about everything thoroughly, but on searching the house they found there were four bedrooms. One their father was using, and the other three had no distinguishing merits. They were all full of junk. The only thing the children had to consider when choosing which room they wanted was which pile of junk was going to terrify them the least when they woke up in the middle of the night, or which pile of junk they were least likely to trip over on the way to the bathroom.

In the end, Joe got the largest room because it had taxidermied animals everywhere. Being the oldest, it was considered he would be the least likely to have nightmares.

April got the room that had a washbasin because she was a girl and therefore the most inclined to wash. (April was a feminist in every regard, except when it came to maintaining sexist stereotypes like boys not washing enough. Although to be fair, she did have evidence to support this belief, having lived with two boys her entire life.)

Fin got the room that overlooked the driveway because he owned a telescope, which the agents had managed to pack for him. He was going to enjoy spying on people approaching the house.

On the whole, the bedrooms were depressing and dusty. But they were separate rooms, so the children were at least pleased that they would each have their own door to slam dramatically when they were fighting.

They went back downstairs to explore the rest of the house. When they returned to the kitchen they were surprised to find their father on his own and clutching an empty mug in his hands, shaking slightly.

'Where's the p-p-professor?' asked Joe.

'Oh, she's gone,' said Dad.

'Just like that?' said April. 'She didn't say good-bye. Typical.' She didn't particularly like Professor Maynard. The whole blowing up their house thing was a lot to get past.

'No, she doesn't often do that,' said Dad.

They all looked at each other. Dad seemed almost as frightened of his children as he did of Professor Maynard. Pumpkin yanked one of Dad's slippers right off his foot. It was old and worn and looked like it smelled gross. Pumpkin was delighted with his new chew toy.

'Would you like me to make some b-breakfast?' asked Joe.

'Oh yes,' said Dad. 'We should eat. Maintaining traditional customs is important.'

Joe opened the food cupboard. There wasn't much to see. Only a lot of tinned food and several enormous boxes of high-fibre breakfast cereal.

'Bran it is then,' said Joe, grabbing a box and looking about for bowls.

A movement in the backyard caught Fin's eye. He went over to the French doors to have a look. 'Am I having a hallucination?' asked Fin. 'Or is there a teenage girl riding a horse in your backyard.'

They all turned to look out the window. The garden at the back of the house was even more impressive than the garden at the front. Huge, exquisitely maintained flowerbeds fanned out between interwoven pathways. It was laid out more like a garden at Versailles than a backyard. And cantering about, weaving among the rainbow of blooms, was an immaculately turned-out chestnut stallion, ridden by a staggeringly beautiful dark-skinned girl with long black hair that swept out behind her in the breeze every time she urged her horse forward to jump over another flowerbed.

'Oh yes, that's Loretta Viswanathan,' said Dad. 'She lives next door.'

The children watched as Loretta's horse misjudged a leap and crashed through a magnificent display of dahlias. Loretta threw back her head and laughed before urging her horse forward again. This time to half-leap and half-crash through a trellis of sweet peas.

'Is she allowed to wreck your garden like that?' asked Joe.

'Well, I've asked her not to,' confessed Dad, 'but she is always so polite and lovely about it. She does come over here fairly often, particularly when there's a show jumping competition she's practising for.'

'But she's a vandal!' exclaimed April.

'A very good-looking vandal,' observed Fin.

Joe turned to look at Fin. He was shocked. Fin had never noticed a girl before.

Fin got defensive. 'What? It's just an empirical fact.'

Chapter 4

SCHOOL UNIFORM

'I'll put a stop to it,' said April menacingly, as she glared at Loretta through the window.

'No, no, no,' said Dad. 'I don't want a confrontation.' He almost looked teary at the thought of it.

'It's not a big deal,' said Fin. 'We'll just go and ask her to stop.'

'But her parents might get upset,' said Dad. 'They're surgeons. Who knows how they might react.'

'What's the worst-case scenario?' asked Fin. 'They take your appendix out?'

'Do you think they would?' asked Dad, genuinely concerned. He started shaking again.

'We can go over and t-t-talk to her later,' said Joe reassuringly. 'Here, you eat your high-fibre breakfast cereal and I'll make you another cup of tea.'

'But there's no time,' said Dad. 'You've got to get ready for school.'

'School?!' exclaimed April. Given that their mother was being held in a secret Kolektiv prison, she had assumed they would get at least one day off school, possibly a month, while they were given lots and lots of trauma counselling.

'Professor Maynard said it is very important that you fit into the community right away,' said Dad, 'to avoid suspicion and questions being asked. She's left uniforms for you in the living room. You're all enrolled. You start at 9 am.'

Joe looked at his watch. 'That's in fifteen minutes! How f-far is the school?'

'A kilometre or two,' said Dad.

'That's only a couple of minutes in a car,' said Fin. 'We'll make it easily.'

'I don't have a car,' said Dad.

'What?!' yelled April. Her father was becoming more and more deeply unimpressive in her eyes. What was the point of a grown-up looking after them if that grown-up didn't have a car to drive them places?

'And we don't have bicycles,' said Joe.

'We did have bicycles,' said Fin, 'until they were blown up with the rest of the house.'

'Okay,' said Joe. 'D-don't panic. We can make it.' He checked his watch again. 'If we rush.'

The Peski kids ran to the living room and hurried to get dressed. But they were not used to uniforms. Their old school's philosophy had been to never stifle a child's self-expression, so students could wear whatever they liked.

'We have to wear ties!' exclaimed Fin, finding a blue tie with gold stripes laid on top of a white shirt. 'Is it even safe to wear something tightly knotted and dangling from your neck? I'm amazed ties haven't been outlawed by occupational health and safety experts long ago.'

'Just put it on,' said Joe. 'You've got to fit in, remember.'

'Humph,' said Fin. 'I suppose I'll fit in perfectly

when it gets caught in a piece of machinery and my head gets ripped off.'

'We're going to school,' said April, 'not a Victorian woollen mill.' But then she was consumed by her own horror. 'Cripes! What on earth is that?!'

April held up the offensive item of clothing. The material was a navy blue and white tartan.

Joe just laughed.

Fin was puzzled. 'What is it?'

Joe sniggered before answering. 'That's a skirt.'

'Nooooooo!' cried April. 'No no no no no no no. I am not wearing a skirt! The suffragettes did not die and endure torture in the fight for women's liberation just so in this day and age I would be forced to wear a skirt!'

Pumpkin started barking and bouncing about excitedly, ready to defend his mistress.

'You've g-got to fit in,' said Joe.

'And please don't rant about feminism on your first day,' pleaded Fin. 'This is a country town. They don't want to hear a twelve-year-old city kid yelling at them about social issues.'

'I won't do it,' said April, dropping the skirt to the floor and plopping down on the couch with her arms folded.

'April, you can't throw a t-t-tantrum now!' pleaded Joe.

'I will not allow myself to be degraded,' said April, turning her head and defiantly staring at the wall. Well, the overflowing bookcase in front of the wall. It didn't really matter, so long as she didn't make eye contact with Joe.

'Our mother is a political prisoner on the far side of the world,' said Fin. 'We're in hiding from counter spies. Our house has been destroyed and we've been driven through the night to get here and ensure our safety. We can't compromise all that. The least you can do is put on a skirt.'

April shook her head. Tears were beginning to well. April rarely cried, unless they were tears of rage. She did that all the time. 'Some sacrifices are too great,' she sniffed.

'On no,' said Fin. He had stopped paying attention to April. He was almost fully dressed, but he was standing still, staring at the last item of clothing.

'What now?' asked Joe.

'Have you seen the hat?' asked Fin. He picked up the strange article. It was blue-and-grey tweed. It looked a bit like a flat cap, except baggier.

'No way,' said Joe.

'Is this some sort of prank?' asked Fin. 'Do we really have to wear one?'

Dad had wandered into the doorway. He was holding their lunches in three brown paper bags.

'Oh yes,' said Dad. 'Currawong High School students all have to wear the famous baggy blue.'

'Huh?' said Fin, so shocked he was reduced to inarticulate grunting.

'Currawong High is famous for being where Roland Guthrie went to school,' said Dad.

The kids just stared at him. This name meant nothing to them.

'Roland Guthrie! The world's greatest lawn bowls player of all time,' explained Dad. 'He wore that distinctive baggy blue cap when he won gold at the Lawn Bowls World Championships seven years in a row.'

'And so n-n-now all the school kids have to wear them?' asked Joe.

'That's right,' said Dad. 'Everyone in Currawong is very proud of the town's lawn bowls history. Except for the people who hate lawn bowls, which is actually most people. But the kids still have to wear the cap, either way.'

'I'm glad I've changed my name and moved miles away,' said Fin, looking down at the cap in his hands. 'At least none of my friends can see me now.'

April scoffed. 'What friends? You never had any friends.'

Fin glowered at April and defiantly jammed the cap on his head. It did not have the effect he had hoped for. Joe and April burst out laughing. Even Dad smiled weakly. Fin had an unusual-shaped head. It was almost pointy, so the cap fell right down to his ears with the brim covering his eyebrows. Given that Fin's ears stuck out and his eyes were beady, altogether it created a rather comic look.

'What? What is it?' demanded Fin. He almost looked bald because the hat completely covered his short hair.

'Nothing,' said Joe. 'Nothing at all.' He put his own hat on and immediately looked like a model for a hat catalogue.

April put hers on backwards and at an angle, making it look both stylish and rebellious. She even put on the skirt. She was still chuckling every time she looked at Fin; it totally made her forget her feminist principles.

'Come on,' said Joe, grabbing their lunches from Dad. 'We'd better run.'

'Wait!' said Dad, as April wrenched open the front door. 'Just remember . . .'

'Kolektiv spies want to kidnap us, we've got it,' interrupted Fin.

'No, I was going to say . . .' Dad was trembling nervously as he fought to find the right words. 'That these people, in town. They're very . . .' He twitched some more. 'Very odd. But they don't realise they're odd. You have to act like they're the normal ones.'

'Okay,' said Joe, patting Dad on the arm. He didn't think his dad was qualified to accuse anyone else of oddness. April and Fin had never had any trouble fitting in at their old school. And Joe liked to be left alone, so not fitting in was fine with him. 'We'll be okay, Dad. Don't worry.'

They took off jogging down the driveway.

———

Pumpkin thought it was excellent that all three of his humans were taking him for a run. The only thing that could top it off would be if there was a nice old lady waiting at the end for him to bite.

They hadn't gone far when suddenly there was a loud HONK behind them. The three kids lurched out of the way. It was a large red car.

'How did we not hear that coming?' asked Joe.

'It's an electric car!' said Fin. 'Their engines are practically silent. They're super swish. I didn't expect to see one of those all the way out here.'

The car had tinted windows so they couldn't see the occupants inside. It didn't speed past as they had expected. It pulled up alongside them and the rear passenger window began to buzz down. Sitting inside was the girl they had seen already that morning, Loretta, their new next-door neighbour.

'Good morning,' Loretta said politely. Up close they could see she was about their age, fourteen or maybe fifteen. Her voice was soft and gentle, with a lovely English accent. 'May I offer you a lift? I'm on the way to school myself.' Loretta was wearing a uniform too, but hers was a different colour and more stylish. She clearly went to a much fancier school.

Fin was again stunned by her beauty. He was just starting to say 'Ye . . .' when he was elbowed out of the way and interrupted.

'No, thank you,' said April. 'We're not allowed to get into cars with strangers.'

'Wait!' said Joe. 'She's n-not a stranger. We know this is L-L-Loretta. Dad told us who she is.'

'We also witnessed her vandalising our father's flowerbeds,' said April.

Loretta chuckled. 'Mr Peski is your father? I didn't realise. Then you must get in. Mr Peski and I are dear friends.'

'He said he's asked you repeatedly not to ride in his garden but you won't stop,' said April.

'Oh, that's nothing,' said Loretta, beaming happily. 'I know Mr Peski doesn't really mean it when he says such silly things. He loves Vladimir.'

'Who's Vladimir?' asked Fin jealously, assuming it was Loretta's boyfriend.

'My horse,' said Loretta. 'Well . . . my jumping horse. Obviously, I have different horses for polo and hack riding.'

'Obviously,' said April sarcastically.

'We'd be very g-grateful for a lift, thank you,' said Joe, hastily getting in the front passenger seat before April could create a scene and offend Loretta.

Loretta slid across the back seat to make room and Fin jumped straight in. April stood and glowered. She would much rather have been late to school than be polite to this unnaturally good-looking girl. But Pumpkin betrayed her by leaping into the back seat and licking Loretta's face.

'What a sweet puppy!' exclaimed Loretta.

'Be careful,' said Fin. 'He bites.'

'*Till den offentliga skolan, tack*, Ingrid,' Loretta called to her driver, an extremely tall, well-muscled blonde woman.

'Huh?' said Joe.

'Don't mind Ingrid,' said Loretta. 'She only speaks Swedish.'

'Your mum only speaks Swedish?' asked Fin.

Loretta laughed again. 'No, silly, Ingrid isn't my mother. She's our au pair.' Loretta leaned forward and tapped Ingrid on the arm before gabbling in Swedish. '*Barnen trodde att du var min mamma.*'

Ingrid burst out laughing. '*Dumma, dumma barn.*'

'What's she saying?' asked April.

'I told her you thought she was my mother,' said Loretta. 'And she said you are stupid, stupid, children.'

'What?' said April, her blood beginning to boil.

'So you're English?' asked Joe, trying to change the subject before April could physically attack Loretta.

'No!' exclaimed Loretta. 'Why ever would you think that?'

'You have an English accent,' Fin pointed out.

'Do I?' said Loretta.

'Yeah, you t-t-totally do,' said Joe.

'No, I was born here,' said Loretta. 'Mummy and Daddy just like me to speak nicely.'

'But where are you from?' asked April.

'Here,' repeated Loretta.

'But,' began April. She looked at Loretta's dark skin and long black hair, stuggling to word her next question without sounding racist.

'Viswanathan is an unusual name,' said Joe, helping his sister out.

'No, it's not,' said Loretta. 'In India it's very common.'

'Your family is from India?' asked Fin.

'No, we're from Sri Lanka,' said Loretta. 'But Mummy and Daddy emigrated. They heard you had a shortage of competent surgeons in this country, so they thought they could make a lot of money by coming here. It turns out they were entirely right. So many people need to be cut open and fiddled with these days. Which is why Mummy and Daddy had to hire Ingrid. They get absolutely no rest at all. They're elbow deep in people's guts all day long.' She leaned forward and spoke to Ingrid. '*Mamma och pappa jobbar för hårt, eller hur?* Ingrid?'

Ingrid snorted.

'What was that?' asked Fin.

'Ingrid was agreeing with me that Mummy and Daddy work much too hard,' explained Loretta.

April scowled. She didn't see how derisive snorting could be taken as agreement.

'What's that?' asked Fin. They were reaching the centre of town and he had just spotted a monstrosity out the window. It was big, brown and lump-shaped. 'It looks like a giant . . .' He couldn't bring himself to say the actual word.

'Poo,' said Loretta helpfully. 'Yes, you're not the first one to notice. It's supposed to be a giant potato. It was built by an eccentric and misguided local farmer who thought a giant potato would make a great tourist attraction.'

'But it's just a huge lump,' said April.

'Yes,' agreed Loretta. 'But it is a tourist attraction. We get three or four tourists a month who stop to have their photo taken with the giant poo.'

'That's disgusting,' said Fin. 'Why hasn't it been taken down?'

'People enjoy the irony,' said Loretta. 'Here we are!'

The car turned into the main street of town.

'So this is Currawong,' said Joe.

There was a bright and cheerful strip of shops. It looked like a tableau from a postcard with the bright blue sky, the rolling hills surrounding the town and the unusual abundance of flower planters overflowing with beautiful blooms. Even the cows in the distant fields looked like they'd been placed there by an artistic director to maximise the beauty of the scene.

'It's so . . . pretty,' said April, as though 'pretty' was a swear word.

'Oh yes, Currawong prides itself on its prettiness,' agreed Loretta. 'We won seventh prettiest town with a population under ten thousand but above five thousand last year in the Eastern Division.'

'I spotted some graffiti!' cried April happily, pointing out the window.

'Where?' asked Loretta.

'On that fire hydrant,' said April. 'It says . . .' She strained to read the rude words but was sorely disappointed. '"Have a nice day"? Who spray-paints nice graffiti?'

'A Currawongian,' said Loretta. 'The town prides itself on niceness too.'

'I think I'm going to be sick,' said April.

'It's just culture shock,' said Fin. 'I'm sure we'll get used to it.'

'Haven't you visited your dad before?' asked Loretta.

'Um . . . n-n-no . . .' said Joe cautiously. He hadn't considered how much they should tell anyone about their past. They probably should have come up with a cover story before they left for school.

'That's odd,' said Loretta, eyeing them shrewdly. 'It never occurred to me that Mr Peski would have children. He's so nervous. I can't even imagine him being married.'

'Yeah, well, h-he was,' said Joe.

'Has your mother come to stay as well?' asked Loretta.

'No, M-M-Mum has been . . . d-d-detained . . . by . . .' Joe trailed off, not wanting to lie, but not wanting to reveal too much either.

'Work commitments,' said Fin, finishing his brother's sentence.

Loretta looked Fin in the eye. He blushed. 'I see,'

she said. 'It sounds like a mystery, and I do love mysteries.'

'No, it's nothing like –' Joe began to protest. But Loretta held up her hand to silence him.

'No, please don't explain. Reality is usually so dull,' she said. 'I'd much rather think of an explanation for myself. I have a very sordid imagination, I'll think up something much better.'

'I bet you don't,' April muttered under her breath.

The car drew to a halt. They were outside the school.

'This is it. Currawong High,' said Loretta. 'Enjoy your first day.'

No one got out immediately. It looked like any other high school in a country town. An old Victorian brick building, surrounded by ramshackle demount-ables that had been incrementally added every decade since. It looked so nice and ordinary that it was intim-idating. The Peski kids were not nice or ordinary. At best they were eccentric, more realistically they were probably weirdos. They had fit in well in their inner city high school. But here, surrounded by flowers and sunshine, they were not so confident they would blend in.

'*Får de dumma barnen ut?*' asked Ingrid, interrupt-ing the silence.

'What did she say?' asked April.

'Ingrid is just wondering if you are ever going to get out of the car,' said Loretta, with a smile.

They opened the doors and stepped out into the sunshine.

'Thank you f-for the ride,' said Joe.

'My pleasure,' said Loretta. 'I'm so pleased to have new children in the neighbourhood. I'm sure we'll get into lots of adventures together. Or have lots of fights and feuds. Either way, it's going to be fun.'

Loretta shut her door and the car whizzed away.

'Well, she's a weirdo,' said April.

'You just don't like her because she's nice,' said Fin.

'I don't trust her because she's nice,' said April. 'She must have some angle.'

'Hospitality?' suggested Joe.

'Pfft,' said April. 'She's probably softening us up for some sort of elaborate initiation prank.'

The Peski kids turned to their new school.

'I suppose we have to go in,' said Fin.

'Well, we'll get sun stroke if we keep standing here,' said April, shoving Fin aside so she could enter the gate first.

Joe and Fin followed in her wake.

Chapter 5

THE NEW SCHOOL

'**Y**ou can't have that in here!' exclaimed Mrs Pilsbury, the school secretary. She was pointing at Pumpkin. April was clutching him protectively to her chest.

'He's my support dog,' said April. 'I need him for medical reasons. I have a doctor's note.'

This wasn't strictly true. April did have a doctor's note, only it was now ashes among the ruins of their house.

Joe, Fin and April were standing in the school's reception area. There was a long high desk with sliding glass windows that separated the secretarial staff from members of the public. It was as if they worked in a bank, except the only thing they had to protect was a bunch of files, a bulk pack of bandaids and their personalised coffee cups, which admittedly they did guard with the protectiveness of a lion defending the carcass of a half-dead antelope.

On the public side of the desk was some worn vinyl furniture and, inexplicably, dozens and dozens of handmade cockroaches dangling from the roof. It was like a sea of incredibly ugly and slightly disturbing piñatas.

'What sort of medical reasons?' demanded Mrs Pilsbury. 'You're not blind, are you?' She peered at April to see if her demeanour gave any hint of bad eyesight. Certainly, April's poorly combed hair indicated that might be a possibility.

'Emotional reasons,' explained April defiantly, holding her chin high. 'Pumpkin helps me cope with my social anxiety disorder.'

'Your what?' asked Mrs Pilsbury.

'Social anxiety disorder,' repeated April.

'You're only a child!' exclaimed Mrs Pilsbury. 'What have you got to be anxious about?'

'Rude adults yelling at me for a start,' said April, glowering at Mrs Pilsbury.

Joe grabbed hold of his sister before she could move any closer. 'April has anger m-m-management issues,' said Joe.

'Her psychiatrist tried counselling, hypnotherapy and medication but none of that worked,' explained Fin. 'So he recommended she get a dog. As you can see, she's still really bad.' April was glaring hatefully at Mrs Pilsbury while hugging a growling Pumpkin. 'But she was way worse before. A dog has really helped her. Of course, Pumpkin bites, so all up about the same number of people get hurt. But now April is only doing half of it herself, so technically it is an improvement in *her* behaviour.'

'You might be able to get away with this malarkey in the city,' seethed Mrs Pilsbury, she was quite good at glaring herself, 'but you're in a small town now. We leave animals in the fields and backyards where they belong.'

'Mrs Pilsbury!' a man with a gentle voice called out. Joe, Fin and April turned to see a podgy middle-aged man in a sweater vest emerging from an office. 'Can I help?'

'This girl has brought a dog to school,' explained Mrs Pilsbury. 'She says her doctor said she can because she's a crackpot.'

'Well, we here at Currawong High School have a charter that requires us to be sensitive to the requests of anybody with mental health special needs,' soothed the man, smiling at the children.

Mrs Pilsbury scowled, sat down on her chair and slid her glass window shut.

'I'll take the children through the orientation process then, shall I?' the man asked Mrs Pilsbury, raising his voice slightly so he could be heard through the glass.

Mrs Pilsbury pretended she couldn't hear him and started loudly typing on her keyboard.

The man turned back to Joe, Fin and April. 'Mrs Pilsbury has been a devoted member of staff here for over thirty years.'

'No wonder she hates children,' said Fin, in his usual matter-of-fact monotone.

'Yes, well, perhaps you'd better come into my office,' said the man.

'Who are you?' asked April rudely, still clutching Pumpkin tightly.

'Sorry, I should have introduced myself,' said the man. 'I'm the guidance counsellor here. You can call me Mr Lang.'

April glared at Mr Lang as if trying to intimidate him purely with her eyebrows. It worked. Mr Lang leaned back instinctively as she strode past him into his office. Joe and Fin followed along.

'Well, your mother's colleague, Professor Maynard has made all the arrangements for you,' said Mr Lang as the children sat down. He moved around to his own side of the desk. 'Joe, April and er . . . I think someone must have written your name down incorrectly,' said Mr Lang, glancing at Fin then squinting at the form in his hand. 'It says here your name is Sharkfin?'

'That's right,' said Fin. 'But I go by Fin.'

'Is this some sort of joke?' asked Mr Lang nervously. 'The higher-ups don't like it when people put jokes on forms.'

'It's not a joke,' said Fin earnestly. 'That's what it says on my birth certificate.'

'But your brother's name is Joe,' said Mr Lang. 'That's quite a contrast.'

'Joe isn't my real name,' said Joe. 'It's P-P-P . . .'

'Peregrine,' April finished for him.

Joe nodded.

'Joe had trouble saying it,' explained Fin.

'Because he's got a stutter,' said April, pointing at Joe so that Mr Lang would know which brother she was referring to. 'It's an involuntary speech disorder where he gets blocked on words.'

'I'm sure Mr Lang knows what a stutter is,' said Fin, rolling his eyes at his sister's insensitivity.

'Well, then he should have said something,' snapped April angrily, 'because it's always better to discuss problems openly and not be embarrassed!'

'I f-f-forged a new birth certificate,' explained Joe.

Mr Lang looked at Joe. He was one of the most ordinary-looking boys he had ever seen. He didn't appear to be the type who could forge a birth certificate, but he supposed young people could do all sorts of surprising things these days with technology. Best not to get into an argument about it. 'All right, well, April and Sharkfin will be going into year 8,' said Mr Lang, handing a timetable to each of them. 'It is a little unusual to have siblings almost a whole year apart in age in the same academic year.'

'Mum couldn't wait to get April out of the house,' explained Fin.

'I could read and do maths already, so Mum packed me off to school with Fin,' said April. 'Everyone assumed we were twins.'

'And you're in year 10 even though you're sixteen,' said Mr Lang, turning to Joe. 'Shouldn't you be in year 11?'

'I got held b-b-back,' said Joe.

'Dyslexia?' asked Mr Lang sensitively.

Fin snorted. 'More like disinterestia,' he said.

'Okay,' said Mr Lang. 'Well, I think the best thing to do is to head to your regular classes and in a week we'll have another meeting to see how you're getting along.'

The kids got up to leave.

'One more thing before you go,' said Mr Lang, opening a drawer and pulling out some more papers. 'You'll need your entry forms for the cockroach races.' He handed one to each of the children.

'The what?' asked Fin.

'The Currawong Annual Cockroach Races,' said Mr Lang. 'Haven't you heard of them?'

'We hadn't even heard of Currawong before yesterday,' scoffed April.

'But we have heard of cockroaches,' said Fin.

'The races are a big deal,' said Mr Lang. 'It's one of our top festivals in town.'

'It's a festival?' asked April incredulously.

'Oh yes, people travel miles to see it. It's wonderful for local tourism,' said Mr Lang. 'It's on next weekend, so you won't have long to train up your entrants. But you can still give it a go.'

'I'm not entering,' said April flatly. 'I don't approve of racing. It's inhumane.'

'C-C-Cockroaches are inhuman,' Joe pointed out.

'Then it's cruelty to animals,' said April. 'I won't have any part of it.' She dropped the form back on the desk.

'But all the students get involved,' said Mr Lang, calling on all his professional levels of patience to maintain his calm and reasonable tones. 'They have a great time.'

'Training animals to compete against each other is not my idea of a good time,' said April. 'I'm amazed no one has reported this to the RSPCA.'

'I'm amazed no one has reported this to a pest controller,' said Fin. 'One spray and there wouldn't be any entrants.'

'How can you be so callous?' demanded April, turning on Fin. 'Cockroaches have feelings too.' Pumpkin started barking and lunging at Fin. 'That's right, Pumpkin, you tell him.'

'Cockroaches are an ancient, simple life form,' said Fin, backing away from Pumpkin's tiny but razor-sharp teeth. 'You have absolutely no evidence that they are capable of higher levels of feeling.'

'Plus they p-poo on food if you leave it out uncovered,' added Joe. He didn't like the thought of food being wasted.

'You should reconsider,' said Mr Lang, raising his voice so he could be heard over Pumpkin's yaps. 'You want to fit in here, don't you?'

'I've never tried to fit in anywhere in my life,' stated April proudly.

'Except that time you tried to fit yourself inside a postbox,' Fin reminded her. 'You managed to squeeze yourself in there all right. It was getting out that was the hard part.'

April did not like it when Fin reminded her of that incident. To punish him, she let go of Pumpkin. Fin ran from the room as the tiny, lightning-fast dog gave chase. April ran after them. If Pumpkin caught Fin, she didn't want to miss that.

'S-S-Sorry,' mumbled Joe, as he picked up his bag.

'Well, you think about it,' Mr Lang called after them. 'When you realise you've made a terrible mistake I'll have the forms here for you.'

Chapter 6

NOT FITTING IN

Joe, April and Fin loitered outside the admin building, consulting their new timetables. Well, Joe and Fin did. April screwed her paperwork up into a ball and used it to play fetch with Pumpkin.

'We've got PE down on the football field,' said Fin.

'Ugh,' said April. 'Let's skip it.'

'You can't skip your f-f-first lesson on your f-f-first day,' said Joe.

'Of course we can!' exclaimed April. 'We can pretend we couldn't find it.'

'How can we not find a football field?' asked Fin. 'It's pretty big and distinctive-looking, plus I can see it from here.'

'I've PE next period, but I've got maths now,' said Joe. He looked like he wanted to cry. He didn't like maths.

'It's not too late,' said April. 'You can make a run for it. I'll get Pumpkin to create a diversion for you.'

'You could homeschool yourself,' said Fin. 'You'd like that. Reading books all day and not talking to anyone.'

Joe nodded. 'But there would be so much f-f-fuss.' Joe hated fuss even more than he hated talking to people. Usually because fuss involved a lot of long and intense bouts of talking to people.

He trudged off towards the maths block. April and Fin ambled in the other direction.

There were thirty students already milling about on the corner of the football field nearest the PE teacher's office. April stood on the bank above the field, hands on hips, surveying her new classmates like an emperor surveying his kingdom. Pumpkin sat at her heels growling, as if waiting for April to signal which one to attack first.

Fin stuck his hands in his pockets, hunched his shoulders and tried to squeeze himself in so that he would appear insignificant and unthreatening, basically as little like April as possible.

'Come on,' said April, nudging Fin. She'd evidently had enough of trying to stare down her peers. 'Let's get this over with. Let's make our first impression.'

'You know, you could try smiling and being nice to people,' said Fin, scurrying along behind her as she strode down the bank.

'Hah!' scoffed April. 'Then they'd think I was weak.'

'People like weak people,' said Fin. 'They make good friends.'

'I don't need to suck up to anyone,' said April. 'I'll just use my normal charm and they'll be eating out of my hand in five minutes.'

'We're doomed,' muttered Fin.

April sidled up and stood next to the rest of the class. Everyone was looking at her, which Fin found mildly relieving. At least his plan to go unnoticed was working. April stared back at her classmates. Her stare was so intense it was as if she were superman, trying to burn a hole in a solid steel wall with her eyes. Several children looked away as she locked her gaze on them. One brave boy spoke.

'You're wearing the wrong uniform,' he said. He was a skinny boy with a lot of freckles, but he apparently had courage disproportional to his size.

'Says who?' asked April menacingly.

'You just are,' said the boy. 'It's the wrong uniform.' He gestured to his own clothes. He was wearing a polo shirt and elasticated shorts, which matched what everyone else was wearing. April and Fin were still in their button-down shirts, leather shoes and, in April's case, the despised skirt.

'Who are you?' asked April, taking a step closer and glaring into the boy's face. 'The uniform police?'

'My name is Darren,' answered Darren literally. 'You can't run around in the regular uniform.'

'Why not?' demanded April, poking the boy in the chest with her forefinger. 'I can do what I like.'

Fin winced. There was going to be a fight or April would taunt the boy until he started crying. Either way, this was not a good first impression.

'But when we do cartwheels and handstands everyone will be able to see your undies,' said Darren.

The rest of the class burst out laughing. The tension had been broken. Fin laughed nervously too. He wanted to be part of the group. April's face went bright red. She looked like she was considering fighting everyone.

'Why do you have a dog here at school?' asked a blonde girl with pigtails, an unusual look for anyone over the age of five. She had the air of a goody-two-shoes about her.

'So I don't have to bite you myself,' threatened April.

'I've got three cattle dogs at home,' called out another boy. 'They'd use your dog as a chew toy.'

The class laughed again. Louder this time.

'Nice one, Kieran,' said Darren, giving the boy a high five.

April's face screwed up with rage. Fin would have grabbed her arm to restrain her, but he didn't want his arm to be broken.

'Get 'em,' she whispered to Pumpkin, and her dog took off like a rocket. Pumpkin leapt straight for Kieran's groin. Kieran jumped back just in time and took off running with Pumpkin close on his heels.

Now April laughed.

'That's enough!' called a man with a thick accent. The class fell silent. The man was wearing a bright red tracksuit, so either he had terrible dress sense or he was their PE teacher.

'We've got new kids,' the pigtail girl called out.

'And they're not wearing the sport uniform,' added Darren.

'Dibber dobber,' sneered April.

'It's just a fact,' said Darren.

'It's just a fact that I'm going to rearrange your face at break time,' said April.

'I'm busy at break time,' said Darren. 'That's when we all play bowls.'

'Huh?' April was getting increasingly confused.

The teacher walked over. He had thick dark hair and a muscly physique.

'I'm Mr Popov, you've heard of me?' he said. It was unclear from his tone whether this was a statement or a question. He had a strange way of speaking in staccato half sentences that were grammatically muddled, as if he were following a pattern from his first language.

'No,' said April rudely.

'I was a boxing champion in my own country,' said Mr Popov.

'I don't approve of boxing,' said April. 'Too many brain injuries. I prefer wrestling.'

Mr Popov glowered. 'Since these students do not bring correct uniform, no sport for anyone today. We do theory.'

The rest of the class groaned.

'That's not fair,' said Fin. 'We didn't know we were going to have PE today.'

'You bring pencils, didn't you? You bring paper?' said Mr Popov. 'Because you know you will be having maths and the English. But always "no" for sport. Always complete surprise you have sport.'

'It's our first day,' said Fin.

'And you no have sport at your old school?' asked Mr Popov.

April was looking in her schoolbag. 'Actually, we don't have pencils or paper either. We came equally unprepared for all our lessons.'

Mr Popov stared at April. 'In my country children do not answer back to teachers.'

'What country is that exactly?' asked April suspiciously.

Mr Popov paused and coloured slightly. 'None of your business. You will be quiet now,' he said. 'I will discuss your attitude with Mr Lang when I see him. Everyone into the classroom.'

The class groaned again.

Mr Popov marched into the room next to his office. The students straggled in after him. 'Thanks a lot, newbie,' whispered the pigtail girl as she walked past. Most of the rest of the class contented themselves with merely glaring menacingly.

April leaned close to Fin. He instinctively flinched away, but she just whispered to him. 'I bet he's a Kolektiv agent.'

'Who?' asked Fin in alarm.

'Mr Popov. He says he's a boxing champion,' said April. 'Why would anyone good at anything want to work here?'

Pumpkin trotted back and proudly dropped a swatch of clothing at April's feet. It looked a lot like the crotch from a pair of boys' gym shorts. There was no sign of Kieran.

'Good dog,' said April, patting Pumpkin on the head.

———

Inside the classroom the students were getting out their pens and paper. Mr Popov had insisted that April tie Pumpkin up outside. She didn't have a leash, so she'd had to make an improvised one out of shoe laces. Not her own, of course; she'd forced Fin to give her his.

'Today we learn about interval training,' said Mr Popov. 'Everyone get out your cockroaches.'

All the other students started rifling through their bags, pulling out shoeboxes, jam jars and Tupperware containers.

'Did he say cockroaches?' asked April.

Fin just shrugged. He was as baffled as her.

'Today you will develop a program to increase the cardiovascular capability of your cockroaches,' said Mr Popov.

The goody-two-shoes pigtail girl put her hand up.

'Yes, what is it, Matilda?' asked Mr Popov.

'The new kids don't have cockroaches,' said Matilda.

Everyone looked at Fin and April.

'What?' demanded Mr Popov. 'No uniforms, no pens and now no cockroaches!'

'Come on!' exclaimed April. 'You can't have expected us to know we needed cockroaches.'

'But the race is this Saturday,' said Matilda.

The other students started muttering to themselves.

'We're not entering the race,' said Fin.

There were several gasps of shock.

Mr Popov sighed. 'Fine, you sit at the back. Observe what everyone else is doing. Just no getting in the way.'

'Aren't we supposed to be learning about *our* physical education, not the physical education of cockroaches?' asked April.

'It's analogous,' said Mr Popov. 'You apply what you learn training cockroaches to your own training.'

'I'm pretty sure this is not in the standardised curriculum,' said April.

'Well, it's in my curriculum!' yelled Mr Popov. 'Go to the back of the class.'

April and Fin watched as the other students broke up into small groups and started running their cockroaches through short exercises. It was all very peculiar. One group encouraged a cockroach to run up the tube of a vacuum cleaner by luring it with a piece of old toast. Another put their cockroach in a clear plastic hamster ball then rolled it around on the floor. And yet another group had a tiny cockroach-sized treadmill made out of a hand-cranked kitchen whisk.

'They're all barmy,' muttered April.

'Nutty as fruitcakes,' agreed Fin. 'But please stop telling them that. We're never going to make any friends if you're not nice to people.'

'I don't want to be friends with a bunch of cockroach lovers,' said April. 'I don't see why we can't go home to the city.'

'Because we'd be killed or kidnapped by Kolektiv agents,' stated Fin.

'Sounds less painful than sitting here watching this,' grumbled April.

At their old school there is no way the students would have cared about cockroach racing. They were all too busy being carted around a myriad of after-school activities. And if there was ever any free time between the yoga, Brazilian jiujitsu and macramé lessons, they would have spent it staring at an electronic device, playing a game or bullying somebody on social media (the most bloodthirsty computer game of all). There is no way they would have spent a split second looking for, catching or training an insect. Let alone a disgusting great big brown one.

After half an hour of experimenting, Mr Popov called his class to order. 'Right, we test your work. Bring your cockroaches to the front.'

Mr Popov rolled out a round mat that was two metres in diameter. Then he produced a large dish with a handle.

'Is that the lid of a wok?' asked April.

'Duh,' said Matilda. 'It's a replica of the official cockroach race ceremonial shield. We're trying to copy race conditions.'

'All competitors under the shield,' said Mr Popov. He raised one edge and the students tucked their roaches underneath. 'All right, on the count of three. One . . . two . . . THREE!'

He whipped back the lid, revealing ten cock-roaches. None of them moved. The students all stared at their roaches intently.

'I can see why everyone finds this such an exciting sport,' said April sarcastically.

'Shhh,' said several people around her.

'We're all just standing here, staring at insects,' said April. 'Why should I "shush"?'

She looked around. Everyone was watching the cockroaches. Some people seemed to be praying, others rocked anxiously and Matilda fiddled nervously with her hand.

'You'll spook the cockroaches,' whispered Darren.

'Puh-lease,' said April, but she was soon interrupted. A cockroach had started to move.

'They're off!' cried Darren.

The rest of the class started screaming too, cries of 'Come on!', 'You can do it!' and 'Run, please run!' echoed around the room.

It was all over in about two seconds. One cockroach made a start, paused, then at lightning speed scurried straight for the outer ring.

'She did it!' exclaimed Matilda, swooping forward and snatching up her roach. She fumbled it into a Tupperware container so quickly she momentarily got her sleeve caught in the lid. 'My Bertha was the fastest!'

'Congratulations,' said Mr Popov.

April snorted. 'Don't congratulate her,' she said. 'She just cheated.'

'How dare you!' exclaimed Matilda.

'I dare because I'm one hundred per cent correct,' said April. 'You cheated.'

'April, please don't do this,' said Fin.

'That cockroach isn't the one that crossed the line,' said April, pointing to the roach scurrying about inside the Tupperware. 'Matilda swapped it out. I saw her. She has another one up her sleeve.'

'That's ridiculous,' said Mr Popov. 'This is just a class exercise. There's no motive to cheat.'

'There is if you want to practise cheating for the big race on Saturday,' argued April.

People were starting to look less contemptuously at April and more contemptuously at Matilda now.

'She's making it up!' accused Matilda. 'She's new and she's got no friends. She's got no proof.'

'But the proof is right there, up your sleeve,' said April. 'The original cockroach must still be in there. I saw you hide something up your cuff.'

'I did not,' said Matilda.

'We'll soon see,' said April. And with that, she finally got to do something physical in physical education. She leapt on Matilda. All the other students stepped out of the way so April had no trouble getting hold of her. Matilda tried to fight her off, but April had a firm grip on her cuff. Eventually both girls pulled so hard, the entire sleeve tore off in April's hands.

'What have we got here?' said April, looking inside. 'Aha!' She pulled out a small plastic tube, the type vitamin tablets come in, and removed the lid. 'A cosy little bedroom for a cockroach.'

April shook it out. The cockroach and a small push-button fell into her hand.

'Hey, that's not a normal cockroach,' said Darren.

'Everything's abnormal here in Currawong,' said April.

'No, there's something not right about it,' said Animesh, a stocky boy whose cockroach had come second in the race.

'Give me a look,' said Fin. He picked up the cockroach. 'It's not a cockroach at all!' he cried. 'It's a robot!'

There were gasps from the rest of the class.

'Look,' said Fin. 'You can see the metal hinges on the legs. And right there is the cover for the battery.'

'And that button is the remote control she used to operate it,' said April.

Matilda burst into tears. 'I'm so sorry. I just really wanted to win.'

'We all want to win,' said Animesh witheringly.

'But my dad won, and his dad won, and his mum won, and her cousin won,' wailed Matilda. 'There's so much pressure to maintain the family tradition.'

'What, were they all cheats too?' asked April.

'I can't be the first person in my family to lose the Cockroach Races since Great-Uncle Waldo,' wailed Matilda. 'He's eighty-one and he's never lived it down. It's haunted him his whole life.'

'That's enough,' snapped Mr Popov. Just then the bell rang, it was the end of class. 'Go on. Get out, all of you. I hope you learned something.'

'I didn't learn much,' said April. 'But to be fair, I learned more than I usually do in PE.'

Chapter 7

JOE AND THE BOWLS

Maths had not gone well for Joe. His teacher had been kind enough, but she was one of those young enthusiastic teachers who still believed in teaching students. So before the lesson began she asked Joe several questions to work out how much he knew about maths. Joe was not a great maths scholar, but even when he knew the correct answer to a question he had the blanket policy of saying 'I don't know.' He found that failing was much less humiliating than trying and failing. And if you said the words often enough, teachers got tired of you and didn't bother asking anymore.

Unfortunately, Miss Willard had a lot of stamina. She didn't give up after three or four questions. She seemed genuinely concerned about Joe's degree of ignorance. She asked no less than twenty-three targeted questions attempting to gauge Joe's amount of knowledge in all the different areas of mathematics. But whether it was algebra, geometry, measuring, long division or even the simple times tables, Joe always answered, 'I d-d-don't know.'

What made it worse, every time he said those words he heard girls giggling and snickering right behind him.

Eventually it occurred to Miss Willard that Joe may have a learning difficulty and that it was cruel of her to keep up the questioning, so she stopped and was just kind, speaking slowly if he looked more confused than normal. For Joe, the kindness made it worse. He knew he was being a coward and letting his nice new teacher down. He wasn't sure which he hated more – maths or himself. He just knew he felt terrible. Like he'd swallowed a brick. He felt sick and heavy.

On the bright side, everyone in his class now

thought Joe was a total moron. So at least he wouldn't have to make small talk at recess. Everyone would avoid him in case dim-wittedness was contagious.

When the bell rang, Joe scraped his stuff into his bag and followed the others down to the oval. No one talked to him along the way. He stared at his shoes so he wouldn't accidentally make eye contact with anyone and see the look of pity in their eyes.

When they arrived at the oval for PE Mr Popov took the roll. 'Nichols . . . Palmer . . . Peski.' His head snapped up. He soon spotted Joe. He was the only one in a tie and collared shirt. Everyone else was wearing their sport uniform.

'Joe Peski?' asked Mr Popov.

'Yes,' said Joe warily.

Mr Popov glared hard at Joe. 'I just had a lesson with your little brother and sister.'

'S-Sorry,' said Joe. No one knew more than him how annoying his siblings could be.

'I'll not put up with any funny business,' snapped Mr Popov.

'Yes, sir,' said Joe.

'Are you being sarcastic?' demanded Mr Popov. He had taught in a public school for fourteen years and no one had ever called him 'sir' before.

'No,' said Joe. 'Just p-polite.'

'Well, cut it out,' warned Mr Popov.

'I thought we weren't in your class today,' said Roger, a tall athletic boy. 'We're with the bowls coach on Tuesdays.'

'I know that,' snapped Mr Popov. 'I wrote the schedule.' He turned on Joe again. 'Now I'm aware that you and your family have no respect for our traditions here at Currawong High School, but it is an honour for us to have a great bowls master like Coach Voss coaching our team. I will not tolerate you showing any disrespect.'

Joe was confused how his attempt at respect had been interpreted as disrespect. April and Fin must have been extremely annoying in their earlier lesson. He was about to say 'Yes, sir,' but he was frightened how Mr Popov would take it so he just nodded instead.

'All right,' said Mr Popov, relenting slightly. 'Give me your shoes.'

Joe was alarmed. He did not like to take his shoes off. He had seriously large feet and he knew people were often startled and stared when they saw them. He glanced across at the girls who had been laughing at him in maths. He couldn't remember when he last cut his toenails. It can't have been any time recently.

The problem with never taking your shoes off is it means that your feet never get a tan, plus the lack of ventilation between your toes can cause fungus to grow, and fungus smells. So the last thing Joe wanted to do, when his classmates already thought he was a nitwit, was take out his giant pale stinky feet.

'Why?' asked Joe. He couldn't imagine Mr Popov's motivation. From the context of the conversation it was as if Mr Popov wanted to keep them as a deposit to ensure Joe's politeness.

'Because they're regular shoes,' said Mr Popov. 'The school gardener, he works tirelessly to ensure the quality surface of our lawn bowls greens. You can't just wander about on them in street shoes. Come on, hand them over. Coach Voss is waiting.'

Everyone in the class was watching Joe now to see what he would do. Joe considered running away, but it would be hard to break through the thirty students standing round him. Plus if you are going to run away from a teacher, it's probably best not to choose your PE teacher. They can most likely run faster than any maths, physics or English teacher.

Joe stood on the back of his left shoe and pulled his foot out. Then did the same with his right. He looked around. Everyone was still watching him. Mr Popov had his arms folded and was tapping his bicep impatiently. Joe bent over and pulled off his left sock. He definitely heard gasps. He pulled off his right sock. This time he could have sworn he heard a girl gag. Joe stuffed the socks in his shoes and handed them to Mr Popov.

Mr Popov took the shoes but he was still staring at Joe's feet. 'Are you good at swimming?' he asked.

Joe looked down. He could see his teacher's line of thought. His feet did look like flippers, but not the elegant type you see on birds or dolphins. His feet were more like the flippers you see on aliens in horror movies that emerge from protoplasmic goo to suck a human's brains out.

'No,' said Joe. This was a lie. He was actually very good at swimming, but he didn't want the PE teacher to start encouraging him or taking him under his wing.

'All right,' said Mr Popov with a shrug. 'You'd better get down to the greens.'

The class shuffled off past the change rooms. As Joe turned the corner he saw two immaculately manicured lawn bowl greens. Unlike everything else at the school that was old and worn down, these greens were clearly lovingly maintained. A bust of Roland Guthrie, former student and lawn bowls champion, stood over the greens as if ready to watch their play.

Standing next to the statue was a man who looked like a statue himself. He was very still and grey. He wore brown cord pants, a short-sleeved collared shirt and a tie with a tie pin. On his head he wore a terry towelling bucket hat. This must be Coach Voss.

The other students grew silent as they approached him. He seemed to capture instant and total respect in the manner you would normally associate with an ancient samurai master. He combined wisdom and a stillness that hinted at great athletic ability despite his age. Coach Voss didn't say anything. He just nodded once. The students clearly knew what this meant. They hurried off, breaking into groups of four and taking out equipment from nearby trunks.

Joe watched, bewildered.

'New?' asked Coach Voss.

Joe nodded.

'Mmm,' said Coach Voss.

Joe waited for him to say more, but it didn't appear likely. Apparently Coach Voss was a man of few words. Joe looked about wondering if he should just copy what everyone else was doing, or if he should make a run for it. Coach Voss was clearly very old. Joe could definitely out-run this teacher.

'Played before?' asked the coach.

Joe shook his head.

Coach Voss pointed at a group of girls nearby who had started playing. 'Bowl the black ball at the white ball.' Joe watched what the girls were doing. He had been tenpin bowling before and this looked like a similar action, only not as aggressive because the ball weighed fifteen kilos less.

'But,' said the coach, holding up his finger to get Joe's full attention. 'The black ball goes in a curve.'

Joe's brow furrowed. That didn't happen at tenpin bowling.

'Try,' said Coach Voss, pointing to a group nearby who only had three players. They looked deflated to be lumbered with Joe, but he went over to join them. Joe watched another boy closely – the way he raised his back hand high before swinging his arm in a pendulum motion, releasing the ball millimetres above the grass.

Joe picked up his own ball, ready to give it a go. He could feel the lop-sided weight that would give it its curve. He looked at the white ball ten metres away, stepped into a lunge, raised his arm back and released.

The black bowl rolled quickly across the perfectly flat grass, arcing away, then back towards the white ball. It slowed more and more until it finally stopped, paused, then fell the last centimetre until it touched the white ball.

Joe stood up and looked around. Everyone was watching him in open-mouthed awe. Coach Voss was right behind him. Joe waited for the coach to speak, but he didn't say a word. He just picked up another bowl and handed it to Joe.

'Again,' said the coach.

Joe turned back to face the white ball and he did it again. He lunged, swung and rolled, and the bowl did the same thing too. It gently arced away then back, slowing down until it came to a stop so it was touching both the white and the other black ball.

When Joe turned around Coach Voss already had another bowl. He held it out to Joe.

'Other way,' he said, handing Joe the bowl so that the weight was on the opposite side.

Joe turned back and bowled. The black ball arced out to the left then back in, slowing down until it stopped on the other side of the white ball. Now all three of Joe's bowls were in contact with it. There was a babble of excitement from the students behind him.

Joe turned to face Coach Voss. The class hushed. They were all waiting to hear what their coach would say.

Coach Voss's lips twitched at the corners ever so briefly, almost as if some of his facial muscles had considered smiling, then thought better of it. Instead he held out his hand. Joe took it. 'Well bowled,' said the coach. Then the rest of the class burst into rapturous applause.

Suddenly everyone was slapping Joe on the back, shaking his hand, even hugging him. Joe had no idea what had just happened.

Chapter 8

DO OVER

'I've had three official complaints about you,' said Mr Lang.

It was after school. April and Fin had been pulled aside in the corridor to talk to the guidance counsellor. Other students were rushing off to catch buses and go to their after-school activities, but Fin, April and Pumpkin were stuck in the corridor, every word of their conversation echoing off the pale blue linoleum.

'But we haven't done anything wrong!' protested April.

'Poor attitude, wrong uniform, physical assault,' said Mr Lang, ticking the complaints off on his fingers.

'We didn't assault anyone,' said April.

'Matilda Voss-Nevers has carpet burn on her face,' said Mr Lang.

'That was only a bit of light wrestling,' said April.

'Her chiropractor says she has strained her shoulder ligaments,' said Mr Lang.

'Well, she was cheating in a cockroach race!' said April. 'You should think about bringing in a team of psychologists. You seem to have a very high level of students with no grasp on reality.'

'They're all nuts,' agreed Fin.

'Yes, I suppose I could try to alter the mentality of all six hundred students at the school,' said the counsellor. 'Alternatively, you two could make an effort to fit in.'

'Come on,' said April. 'You can't expect us to change when everyone here is totally cracked!'

'If you moved to a school in a different country, you would respect the local culture and traditional customs,' said Mr Lang calmly. 'It's just polite. You should do the same here.'

'To be fair,' said Fin. 'April wouldn't be polite or respectful anywhere.'

'And then there's your dog. You have to keep him under control,' continued Mr Lang.

'Pumpkin is perfectly behaved!' argued April.

Pumpkin immediately contradicted this by grabbing hold of Mr Lang's trouser leg and tearing a hole in the fabric when the counsellor tried to shake the dog off.

'He's very protective,' said April. 'Aren't you, sweetheart?'

Pumpkin proudly allowed himself to be patted.

'Your brother Joe hasn't had any trouble fitting in,' said Mr Lang. 'Coach Voss says he's the most naturally talented lawn bowler he's ever seen, which is actually the most I've ever heard Coach Voss say. Not a chatty man.'

'What?' said Fin. 'Joe has managed to fit in?'

'The kids here have a lot of respect for sporting prowess,' said Mr Lang.

'Joe has prowess?!' marvelled Fin.

'But lawn bowls isn't a real sport,' said April. 'It's just for old people.'

Mr Lang's eyes gaped in horror. 'Shhh, don't say that. Someone might hear you.'

'Yeah, yeah,' said April, waving her hand dismissively. 'Look, I like Joe because he's my brother.'

'You do?' said Fin. 'You've never liked me.'

'You're more annoying,' said April. 'But I can't imagine how Joe would be popular. He's just a big lunk. And he smells. I know all teenage boys smell, but Joe smells more because he's so big there's more of him to be smelly.'

The counsellor opened his folder and took out the entry forms again. 'Just enter the cockroach races. It will do you good. You'll get to know the other students. They'll get to know you. You'll have a shared interest.'

'But . . .' began April.

'No buts!' snapped the counsellor. Pumpkin growled. The counsellor glared back and Pumpkin went quiet. 'We tried doing things your way. It didn't work. Now we're doing things my way. Fill out the forms, hand them in at the front office, then go home and catch yourself a cockroach. That's an order.'

April stared at Mr Lang mutinously. She had never attempted wrestling a school staff member before, but she was considering giving it a shot.

Fin reached forward and took both forms.

'Come on,' he said. 'We can't let Joe be more popular than us. He'll be gracious and kind about it. And that will only make it worse.'

Chapter 9

THE FIRST HURDLE

When they got home April and Fin set to work looking for cockroaches. It was a lot harder than they imagined. They searched down the back of the kitchen cabinets, pulled out the kickboard and even dragged out the refrigerator from the wall so they could look behind it. Nothing. They did find a spider but it didn't last long because Pumpkin ate it.

'I thought there were supposed to be thousands of cockroaches in every home,' said April.

'They're just good at hiding,' said Fin. 'They're thigmotropic.'

'What does that mean?' asked April.

'They like to be touching as many surfaces as possible,' said Fin. 'So they squeeze themselves into tiny spaces. I read somewhere that they particularly like to live inside microwaves.'

'But they'd be cooked,' said April.

'Only in the oven part,' said Fin. 'Inside the panelling it's nice and warm, there's lots of delicious cooking grease nearby and there are loads of crevasses to hide in.'

April looked at their father's microwave. She had an evil gleam in her eye. 'Let's open it up.'

'Do you think Dad will mind?' asked Fin.

'Only if he notices,' said April. 'He's been shut in his office since we got home from school. We could be testing a thermonuclear device in here and he wouldn't know about it.'

'Of course he wouldn't,' said Fin. 'If we were testing a nuclear device, he'd be dead from the radiation poisoning.'

April was already rifling through the cutlery drawers, looking for something she could use to prise open the microwave. Fortunately, their father was not good at cooking, so he kept a lot of mechanical tools in them. April soon found a variety of screwdrivers, spanners and pliers, but the implements she took up were a chisel and heavy mallet.

'Are you sure that's a good idea?' asked Fin, as he watched his sister start attacking the microwave.

'No,' said April, panting between heavy blows of the mallet. The metal began to buckle under the point of the chisel and the plastic fronting soon tore away and cracked. April grabbed hold of this and pulled, completely separating the digital keypad from the backing.

They both peered at the electronics within.

'Can you see anything?' asked Fin.

'Just the inside of a microwave,' said April.

'What are you doing?' asked Dad, bursting into the kitchen and startling April and Fin. 'Did you find a listening device in the microwave? Or a hidden camera?' He dropped his voice to a whisper. 'Is someone watching us?'

'Um, I'm tempted to say "yes",' said April.

'We're looking for cockroaches,' said Fin. 'We need one to enter in the cockroach races.'

Their father looked horrified. He staggered back a step. 'Cockroaches!' he exclaimed. 'There are none in this house. I have it thoroughly sprayed four times a year by pest controllers.'

'Isn't that a bit excessive?' asked April. 'I don't think Mum ever had our house sprayed.'

'They're horrible disease-carrying creatures,' said Dad. 'I won't have them here!'

'But you're a gardener,' said April. 'Aren't you used to bugs?'

'I hate them all,' said Dad. 'Aphids eat my roses, centipedes destroy my strawberries and butterflies are a nightmare.'

'Butterflies are pretty,' said April, who wasn't usually a connoisseur of beauty, but even she could appreciate they were nice.

'Butterflies are the worst!' exploded Dad. 'They destroyed the new growth on my citrus last autumn.'

'Okay,' said Fin, patting his dad comfortingly on the arm. 'Why don't you go back to your office? We'll reconstruct the microwave, then bring you a nice cup of tea. You just relax. Have a nap.'

'You didn't find any cockroaches, did you?' worried Dad. 'I can't sleep if there's one in the house.'

'No, not one,' said Fin. 'You must have an excellent pest controller.'

'She is very thorough,' agreed Dad. 'I have to wear a respirator for a week after she's been because the house smells so bad.'

They watched Dad leave.

'I told you he wouldn't notice if we took apart the microwave,' said April.

'Only cause he's bonkers. What are we going to do?' asked Fin. 'Once we find a cockroach, we'll have to bring it back here. He'll freak out.'

'We'll worry about that later,' said April. 'First we need to find a cockroach. Let's go and meet the neighbours. Maybe one of them will have lower hygiene standards than Dad.'

———

Fin, April and Pumpkin went over to their next-door neighbour's house. The property had a long tree-lined driveway, just like their own, but that is where the similarity ended. When they got to the top and the trees opened out, a magnificent mansion came into view. It was nothing like their own humble home. This house was new and clean and shiny. It looked like a home from an interior decorating magazine. It was almost too good to live in. Of the three of them, only Pumpkin wasn't intimidated. He did a poo in the middle of the perfectly manicured lawn.

Fin and April had known rich people in the city, but no one rich enough to own a house like this. Asking a normal person if they had cockroaches was hard, but asking a super-rich person who lived in a beautiful mansion if their home was pest-infested might just sound rude.

'You knock,' said Fin nervously.

'No, you do it,' said April, stuffing her hands in her pockets to make them inaccessible. She didn't like following orders.

'You do it,' said Fin. 'You're closer.'

'We're exactly the same distance away,' said April.

'Just knock on the door,' said Fin, stepping back. 'You're taller, so it's easier for you.'

'You're older, you should take the leadership role,' said April.

'People like girls better,' said Fin. 'You should do it.'

'Don't you start your gender bias on me!' exclaimed April, turning on her brother. Pumpkin ran over barking, sensing a fight was about to break out.

In the end, neither of them knocked. When the door opened a minute later, April had Fin in a headlock and was trying to give him a wedgie while Fin tried to fight April off by whacking her with her own shoe. Pumpkin was hanging off the back of Fin's jumper by his teeth.

'Hello!'

They glanced up. It was Loretta. She looked even more beautiful than she had that morning. She was dressed for riding now, wearing long shiny boots, tight jodhpurs and a flowery blouse.

'We didn't knock,' said April, confused.

'I know,' agreed Loretta. 'But you set off the intruder alarm. The security firm that monitors the hidden cameras rang, advising me to put the house in lockdown, but I was ever so curious to see who the intruders were, so I opened the door.'

'We didn't mean to bother you,' said Fin.

'I can see that,' said Loretta. 'Clearly you're busy.'

April let Fin out of the headlock and he straightened his shorts while returning April's shoe. Pumpkin let go of Fin's jumper and dropped onto the gravel driveway so he could run over to Loretta for a pat.

'The reason we're here,' said Fin, 'is we're looking for a cockroach.'

'You're going in the races!' exclaimed Loretta, clapping her hands with delight. 'How marvellous!'

'You're going in them too?' asked April.

'Oh yes,' said Loretta. 'I enter every year. I got Daddy to ship over a Madagascan hissing cockroach. It arrived two days ago. She's huge. I think she will be a good racer.'

'We need to get one,' said Fin.

'The race is five days away,' said Loretta. 'You don't have time to order one online. You'll have to find a normal cockroach. That's what most kids do anyway.'

'We don't mean to be rude, but do you think you might have any here?' asked Fin. 'Dad is overzealous with pest control, so there are none at our place.'

'I'm sure there must be,' said Loretta, waving them into the house. 'Let's have a look.'

Fin, April and Loretta spent over an hour searching for a cockroach. Loretta very kindly let them rifle through the whole house. She didn't even make them take their shoes off before walking on the expensive Persian carpets, the pristine polished marble floors or the impeccably ironed linen bedding. They'd spent quite a lot of time standing on the master bed because it was the only way they could pull down the cut-glass light fitting to see if there were cockroaches inside.

Eventually – after dismantling the state-of-the-art stainless steel microwave in the designer gourmet kitchen, then putting it back together with sticky tape – April and Fin had their roach. She looked like a normal, ordinary cockroach, but it had taken a long time to catch her as she scurried about the kitchen floor desperately trying to escape, so they had great hopes she would make a top racer.

'Well done,' said Loretta. 'What are you going to call her?'

'You name your cockroaches?' asked April.

'Of course,' said Loretta. 'The commentator has to yell out something when they take the lead.'

'There's a commentator?' asked Fin. 'So people take these races pretty seriously then?'

'Oh my word, yes,' said Loretta. 'There's a commentator, a referee, an official weigh-in and a camera crew.'

'What's the camera crew for?' asked April.

'The races are televised,' said Loretta.

'No way!' said Fin.

'Yes way!' said Loretta. 'It's very popular. People watch them all around the world. They love it in Japan. We had a Japanese team enter a couple of years ago, but they misunderstood the rules. Apparently in their country there is a game show were people put cockroaches down their pants. Several contestants were lost before we could get hold of a translator to explain that wasn't the way we played the game here in Currawong.'

'You're kidding,' said Fin.

'Oh no,' said Loretta. 'It's televised across India as well, but then most things you can gamble on are televised in India.'

'People gamble on cockroach races?' exclaimed April incredulously.

'Of course,' said Loretta. 'I don't see how that is any harder to believe than betting on horses or greyhounds. In fact, it makes much more sense. Cockroaches are far cheaper to keep. And it's easy to televise because the race takes place in a two-metre-wide circle, so you only need one camera. When you think about it, it's amazing it hasn't taken off in more places.'

'Thank you for letting us look for a cockroach in your house,' said April begrudgingly. She didn't like being grateful to anyone, especially someone so beautiful and charming, but it had been kind to let them search the splendidly decorated house.

'Yeah, and if you have any problems with the microwave, let me know,' said Fin. 'I'm good at fixing things.'

'Oh, this isn't my house, or my microwave,' said Loretta.

'Of course, it's your parents' house,' said Fin. 'But thank you anyway.'

'No, it's not their house either,' said Loretta.

'But you live here,' said Fin.

'No, I live in the house on the other side of yours,' said Loretta. 'The big blue one with the more modern architecture.'

'Then whose house is this?' asked April.

'Mrs Sherman,' said Loretta. 'She works in the city during the week. She's a terribly important lawyer, or judge, or something to do with sending people to jail. Actually, I think technically she's Justice Sherman. She does keep asking me to call her that.'

'Then why are you in her house?' asked Fin. 'Do you come over to water the plants?

'No,' laughed Loretta. 'I break in for fun.'

'You're yanking our chain!' said April incredulously.

'It's true,' said Loretta. 'These people who buy weekenders are never here. Not even on weekends

111

because they're always too busy. It's fun breaking in and looking at their stuff. Mrs Sherman has a lovely grand piano. It's a lot of fun to play. Miss Smith across the road always has chocolate in her pantry, and Salman down the road loves vacationing in Europe, which gives me lots of time to go over and swim in his pool.'

April squinted at Loretta. She wasn't sure if she was joking. She didn't look at all like the sort of person who would break into houses. She was much too neat and pretty for a start. If April broke into a house, she would look like she'd been pulled through a hedge backwards.

'Don't you have a pool?' asked Fin.

'Of course,' said Loretta, 'but Salman has a better jacuzzi.'

'What about the security system?' asked Fin.

Loretta laughed. 'That's the funny part. Mrs Sherman is forever overseeing murder trials, so she should know all about how devious criminals are, and yet in her own house the security code is 1234. Can you believe it? 1234! I was all prepared to hack the security company's mainframe but there was no need.'

Chapter 10

SOMETHING IN THE BUSHES

Dad was fast asleep in his office. He could never sleep at night. He was too scared. That's when the bad dreams would come. But for some reason, when he sat as his desk with a huge pile of work to get through on a warm afternoon – he could sleep like a baby.

He was dreaming about a Venus flytrap. It kept growing bigger and bigger. Then, when he looked down, he realised he was standing inside the plant's jaws. He tried to escape but the jaws had been triggered and they were snapping shut. He couldn't push through the teeth. When he looked up, the leaves of the plant were folding over him, ready to kill, but then the leaves transformed into his wife and the teeth were samurai swords swishing through the air towards him.

'Waaaghh!' cried Dad. A noise had woken him up. His first thought was of his wife, but then he remembered she was in jail on the other side of the world. He knew he shouldn't be relieved, but he was. Then he remembered that there were other people out there almost as scary. Kolektiv agents who wanted to kill him.

Dad heard the noise again. It was faint, but definitely a whirring, like a power drill. Dad leapt to his feet. He was too terrified to confront anyone, but he was brave enough to go and see if he needed to run away.

Dad crept over to the window. He couldn't see anything. As quietly as possible he pushed up the sash and leaned out. There was nobody there. Then his eye caught a movement at the far end of the garden.

He could have sworn he saw a foot disappear into a hedge. Dad started to tremble. Someone had been there. What were they doing? What did they want? If they were going to kill him, why didn't they do it?

Dad awkwardly climbed out of the window to have a closer look. Perhaps he had imagined it. His psychologist had told him he had an overactive imagination. Perhaps the whirring wasn't a drill, it was the wind. And perhaps the movement in the bushes was just a rabbit or some other wild animal. Dad couldn't see any alteration to the outside of the house. Then he noticed something. Something tiny on the grass right by the house. He crouched down to get a closer look. There was a very small pile of sawdust, as if someone had drilled a hole in the side of the house.

Dad ran his hands along the walls, taking his time to thoroughly search, but he couldn't find a hole. What did that mean? Had someone drilled a hole, then filled it? This was going from bad to worse.

Chapter 11

KITTY-CAT BANDAIDS

Joe let himself in the front door and headed for the kitchen, where he found his dad crouching behind the kitchen sink. He was peering out through the venetian blinds.

'Hey, Dad,' said Joe, as he dumped his schoolbag by the kitchen counter.

Dad jumped with fright. 'Aagghh!'

'It's only m-m-me,' said Joe. 'Where are April and Fin?'

'What?' said Dad, suddenly alarmed. 'They're not here?'

Joe looked about. 'I can't see them.'

'They were here half an hour ago,' said Dad, looking out the window as if a Kolektiv hit man might be lurking among the daisies. 'You don't suppose they've been kidnapped?'

'They're probably doing something out in the yard,' said Joe, walking over to the cupboard to grab a bag of popcorn. He stopped when he saw the microwave. 'What happened?'

The microwave was back on the counter and it had been reassembled, but the metal casing was warped and the plastic panel at the front was only held on by kitty-cat bandaids.

'I don't know,' said Dad. 'Do you think someone broke in and tampered with it?'

'I don't think a secret agent would do such a bad job,' said Joe, 'or use such pretty b-b-bandaids to put it back together. This looks more like April's handiwork.'

'She was doing something with a mallet earlier,' Dad remembered vaguely.

Joe put the popcorn in the microwave and turned it on. The microwave started up, the light came on and the dish started turning. 'Hey, it still works. Cool!'

The front door slammed.

Dad gasped and ducked under the kitchen counter. 'It's the Kolektiv! Hide!'

'Hello,' called Fin.

Pumpkin barked.

'It's just April and Fin,' said Joe.

Dad clutched his chest. 'What a relief! There was someone in the garden earlier today. I'm pretty sure it was an international secret agent come to kidnap you all.'

Joe looked out into the garden. Aside from the horse jumping damage, the flowerbeds were beautiful. It didn't look like the type of place international operatives would work.

'You know, Dad, perhaps you should cut back on the caffeine. Swap to chamomile tea,' said Joe. 'You'd be less jumpy.'

Pumpkin rushed in and bit Dad on the ankle.

'Ow!' yelled Dad.

As soon as April saw Dad she whipped her hands behind her back.

'What have you g-got there?' asked Joe.

'Mind your own business, big nose,' said April.

Dad looked at Joe. His son didn't have a particularly large nose, so this expression confused him.

'Big head more like,' said Fin. 'You must think you're pretty good now that you're the big man at school.'

This confused Dad further. Joe was a large man-sized boy, but he didn't understand how his size could alter when he was at school.

Joe blushed. 'It's not my f-f-fault I've got a knack for it.'

'A knack for what?' asked Dad, afraid his son was going to say hand-to-hand combat or something equally horrifying.

'Lawn bowls,' said Joe.

'He's an idiot at it,' said April.

'You mean "idiot savant",' corrected Fin.

'You say tomato, I say tomato,' said April.

'You shouldn't call your brother names,' chided Dad.

'I don't see how "idiot" became such a bad word,' complained April. 'All the other words for "idiot" are much worse.' She kicked Fin in the shin to get his attention. 'Why don't you show Dad something in your schoolbag?' She waggled her eyebrows meaningfully.

Fin looked confused. 'Why would I do that?'

'Because I'll punch you if you don't,' said April, glancing back behind her and twitching the box with the cockroach so only Fin could see it.

'Oh!' said Fin, catching on. 'Right. Dad, here have a look at . . . my um . . . lunchbox! It's really important for parents to know what their kids do and don't eat.'

While Dad was distracted, April walked over to a large domed terrarium Dad had on the kitchen windowsill where he grew herbs. She checked over her shoulder to see that Dad wasn't looking.

'But you've eaten everything,' Dad observed, peering into the lunchbox. 'There's nothing to see.'

'I know,' said Fin. 'And look, here is a tissue I blew my nose on at recess.'

April dumped the cockroach in the terrarium.

'Fascinating,' said Dad, looking at the tissue. 'And you kept this just to show me?'

'If we're going to build a meaningful father-son relationship,' said Fin, 'it's important to start with the little things.'

April hurried away, but a movement caught Dad's eye.

'Did you see that?' he exclaimed, pointing to the window. For one horrifying moment April and Fin thought he had spotted the cockroach, but Dad rushed to the kitchen drawer and pulled out a pair of military-grade binoculars, then trained them on something distant out the window.

'See what?' asked Fin.

'Something moving in the bushes! At the far end of the garden,' said Dad.

'You mean the wind?' said April.

'You stay here, I'm going to check it out.' Dad scurried to the back door, let himself out, then commando crawled through the maze of flowerbeds towards the back hedge. Pumpkin happily chased after him, barking and biting Dad on the leg excitedly as he went.

The Peski kids stood at the kitchen window, watching him go.

'Do you think Dad is nuts?' asked Fin.

'Beyond a shadow of a doubt,' said Joe.

'Should we get him some sort of professional help?' asked Fin.

'He's just been living alone for too long,' said Joe. 'He'll probably calm d-d-down when he's used to having us about the house.'

'Besides,' said April, 'these wild conspiracy theories do him good. Look, he's outdoors enjoying the sunshine, playing with the dog.'

Dad was now running around in circles with Pumpkin delightedly hanging off the back of his pants.

'If there was someone hiding in the hedge,' said Fin, 'the sight of that would scare them off as effectively as anything else.'

Chapter 12

PAPER, ROCK, GLASS

Fin was lying in bed, happily dreaming about robots that dispensed chocolate, when somewhere in the back of his mind he became aware of a tapping sound. It wasn't a frequent tap. There was no pattern. Just a tap, a long pause, then another tap. It sounded almost as if something was hitting a sheet of glass. Something small like a pebble. Then suddenly – CRASH!

Fin sat bolt upright. Broken glass was littered all over his bed and a large rock was lying on his bedroom floor. His first instinct was to run to the door and get out of there, but there was broken glass everywhere and he had bare feet, so he hesitated. Then he heard a very pleasant feminine voice call out, 'Yoo-hoo, is anybody home?'

Fin reached for his sneakers, jammed them on, then went over to the window. It was pitch black outside. Suddenly, something small and hard hit him in the middle of his forehead.

'Ow!' cried Fin.

'Oops, sorry,' said Loretta. Fin could see her in the dark. She was holding a flashlight.

'You threw a pebble at my head!'

'I didn't know your phone number,' said Loretta.

'And you smashed my window with a rock,' said Fin.

'Well, the small pebbles weren't waking you up,' reasoned Loretta.

'What do you want?' asked Fin.

'Help,' said Loretta. 'I've got a problem. And it's really serious.'

Fin's heart swelled in his chest. This was it. This was his moment. He would get to be a knight in shining armour. There was literally a damsel in distress coming to him and asking for help.

'Don't worry,' said Fin bravely. He tried to make his voice a little deeper than usual, to sound more impressive. 'I'll save you.'

Just as his dream seemed about to come to fruition, a nightmare unfolded before his eyes. Something shot across the front lawn. There was a terrifying scream of 'Hiiiiyaaaahhh!' followed by another terrified scream of 'Aaaaaggghh!' as April flew through the air and crash-tackled Loretta to the ground. All while Pumpkin bounded around them both, barking.

'I got her!' called April happily.

'What are you doing?' cried Fin, horrified to see the most beautiful girl he had ever known in real life pinned beneath his violence-prone sister.

'She smashed your window,' said April. 'I heard it. I snuck out to catch her before she ran off. You're welcome, by the way.'

'She came to ask for help,' said Fin.

'Is that true?' asked April.

'Yes,' said Loretta, trying to brush the dirt out of her mouth.

'Why did you break the window then?' asked April.

'He didn't wake up when I threw a pebble,' said Loretta.

'That would be right,' said April, helping Loretta up. 'He sleeps like the brain dead.'

Just then Joe arrived in Fin's room. Even in the moonlight he could see that there was broken glass all over the floor. But he had shoes on, so he crunched over to the window and saw April trying to brush off a very dishevelled Loretta.

'What's g-g-going on?' asked Joe.

'I need you to come over to my house, right away,' said Loretta.

Chapter 13

SOMETHING SERIOUS

Loretta led the way across the Peski kids' garden, through a hole in the fence, which looked like it had been made recently with a chainsaw, and into her own yard.

'You'd better whisper from now on,' said Loretta, as they pushed through a dense thicket of bushes.

'Why?' asked Fin. 'This is *your* garden, isn't it?'

'Of course, silly,' said Loretta. 'But Mummy and Daddy are paranoid about burglars, so they're likely to shoot first and ask questions later.'

'They've got g-g-guns?' asked Joe.

'Oh no, they could get in trouble with the medical practitioners board if they shot someone with a gun,' said Loretta. Joe looked relieved. 'They've got tranquiliser darts,' she added, 'and capsicum spray. The type you get in Mexico that, I'm pretty sure, isn't legal here.'

Eventually they emerged onto a lawn and saw Loretta's actual home. It was magnificent. It looked like an architect had been given a great deal of money to come up with a dwelling that would be appropriate for a settlement on Mars. There were very few right angles, just lots of domes and curved glass walls. Not the type of thing you'd expect to see when you push through a vandalised fence and a hedge in a small country town.

'Cutting people open must pay well,' commented April.

'It's r-r-rude to talk about how much money people earn,' chided Joe.

'Oh, it's no secret,' said Loretta. 'Mummy and Daddy are loaded. Doctors get paid squillions. Then they invest that and get squillions more. In fact, some of their investments were a little shady, which is why they had to spend so much on the house. A couple of years ago the tax department was targeting coronary surgeons with offshore bank accounts, so they needed to get rid of a lot of cash quickly.'

Loretta led the way around the side of the house.

The Peski kids assumed they were heading to the front door, but Loretta stopped suddenly next to the wall.

'This way,' she said, as she grabbed hold of a drain-pipe. Then, with surprising agility, she scrambled quickly up it to an open window on the second floor.

The other three stood and stared.

April was the first to respond. 'Okay,' she said, with a shrug. Then she shoved Pumpkin inside her jumper and scrambled up herself, grabbing the lintel and vaulting into the room.

Joe held the downpipe and gave it a little shake. It was PVC. He wasn't confident it would take his greater weight. 'Y-You first,' he indicated to Fin.

Fin gaped. He was not athletic or agile, and he had very little upper-body or grip strength. He silently begged his brother with his eyes to forbid him to do this, but Joe was not fluent in silent eye language, particular when it was dark and he couldn't really see the eyes that were appealing to him.

Fin swallowed hard, grabbed the drainpipe and tried to shinny up, the same way April and Loretta had. After a flurry of exhausting activity, he stopped to rest. He looked down to see that he was only two feet off the ground. At this point, Joe took pity on his brother. He put his hand firmly on Fin's butt and pushed him up as high as he could reach. Fin was then able to stretch across and grab the windowsill. From there he scrambled inelegantly inside.

'Couldn't you just let me in through the f-f-front door?' Joe asked Loretta.

'Oh no,' said Loretta. 'Mummy and Daddy wouldn't like that. They don't like me having friends over. Particularly late at night. And particularly not boys. They're very judgemental about boys.'

Joe weighed up the pros and cons of being caught by two tranquiliser-gun-wielding surgeons in their daughter's bedroom. It didn't seem worth the risk.

Up in the bedroom Pumpkin barked loudly. There were responding barks from not far away, but these barks sounded like they came from much bigger dogs.

'I wouldn't stand there though,' said Loretta. 'The Dobermans have just woken up and they're trained to bite intruders.'

The barks were getting louder. Joe could hear the dogs running through the bushes. Suddenly, two hounds burst out on the other side of the lawn. They didn't look like regular dogs, they looked like wild beasts of prey ruthlessly running down their dinner in the wild jungle. Joe did not hesitate. Adrenaline surged through his body. He jumped and grabbed the windowsill, pulling himself up. He was soon sprawled upside down on the floor of Loretta's bedroom.

'Well done,' said Loretta.

Joe looked about. Loretta's room was amazing. Everything was either white or pink, and he had never seen so many unicorns in his life. There were stuffed unicorns, paintings of unicorns, model unicorns hanging from the ceiling, a unicorn bedspread and unicorn-patterned curtains.

'You like unicorns, huh?' said Joe, trying to be polite when really he was shocked. He knew stereotypically girls were meant to like pink fluffy unicorns, but growing up with April he had never actually witnessed this level of unicorn worship through interior decoration before.

'No,' said Loretta, chuckling. 'They're very silly, but Daddy likes to think I like unicorns, and I like to keep Daddy happy. It makes him less observant of my other interests.'

'Like housebreaking,' said Fin.

Loretta laughed. 'Oh no, that's the least of it.'

'Blah blah blah,' said April rudely. 'You've dragged us all over here on a school night when we should be asleep, so how about we get on with it. What's your problem?'

Loretta grew sombre. 'There's been a murder!'

The other three stared at her. Murder was obviously very serious, but Loretta didn't look devastated, which was confusing for them.

'Did you do it?' asked April.

'Of course not!' said Loretta.

'Who's d-d-dead?' asked Joe. He was the one with closest to normal human emotions, and he was very concerned by the turn of the conversation.

'Mr Bottomley,' said Loretta.

'Is that a teacher at your school?' asked April. She didn't know anyone other than teachers who still had to be referred to as 'Mr'.

'No, Mr Bottomley means much more to me than that,' said Loretta. Her eyes began to water and she bit her lip. 'He's my *Gromphadorhina portentosa*.'

'Your what?' asked Joe.

'My Madagascan hissing cockroach,' said Loretta. 'Come and see.'

She led them over to two large doors in the far wall of the room. The Peski kids assumed it was a walk-in wardrobe, but when Loretta threw open the doors they were in for a shock. Clothes took up only a fraction of the space. The rest of the wardrobe looked like an evil villain's lair. There were monitors showing live feeds from security cameras, a whole chemistry set-up where a strange green liquid was bubbling away and a pegboard on which hung a wide variety of power tools and even a couple of things that looked like weapons.

'Cool,' said April, as she reached for a slingshot.

'Mr Bottomley lives over here,' said Loretta. In one corner of the wardrobe there were three aquariums. One was full of water and contained fish.

'Is that a piranha?' asked Fin, looking at the unusually large teeth on one of the fish.

'Not at all,' said Loretta with a wink. 'It's illegal to keep piranha in this country.'

In another aquarium there was an enormous black snake coiled up in the bottom corner. But the third aquarium appeared to be empty. There were only a few rocks and plants.

'What are we looking at?' asked Fin.

Loretta just pointed.

Under the leaves there was a large brown shiny lump. At first glance Fin had assumed it was a rock. But it wasn't.

'That's a cockroach?!' exclaimed April.

'It's huge!' exclaimed Joe. It was twenty times larger than Fin and April's cockroach.

'They're bred as pets,' said Loretta. 'They're very affectionate and they hiss in the most charming manner.'

'Are you sure it's dead?' asked Fin. 'I've heard about cockroaches being frozen in snow, then waking up when the snow thaws as if nothing happened.'

'It's twenty-one degrees in the tank,' said Loretta, pointing to a thermometer stuck to the side of the aquarium. 'How could he have frozen?'

'He could be st-st-stunned,' said Joe.

'Cockroaches are covered in chitin,' said Loretta. 'In terms of surface area to volume ratio they are better protected than an armoured personnel carrier. What on earth could stun him?'

'It definitely looks dead to me,' said April, tapping

the side of the clear glass. 'Lying on its back with its legs in the air is a pretty compelling set of symptoms.'

'Perhaps he died of old age,' said Fin.

'Don't be ridiculous,' said Loretta. 'Madagascan hissing cockroaches live up to five years in captivity. Mr Bottomley was only four months old and he was in perfect health when we bought him two weeks ago. I have a certificate proving that from the breeder and an independent vet who checked him.'

'What about natural causes?' said Fin. 'Perhaps he picked up a disease.'

'How could he pick up a disease?' asked Loretta. 'Cockroaches spread disease, they don't catch them themselves. Besides, he's the only Madagascan hissing cockroach in a five-hundred-kilometre radius. There are no other cockroaches of his species that he could have caught a disease from.'

'So you suspect foul play?' April leaned in to get a closer look at Mr Bottomley. Pumpkin leaned in as well, but he was thinking more about whether the brown shiny lump would taste good.

'Could it have been your parents?' asked Fin. 'If our dad found a cockroach in an aquarium, I'm pretty sure he'd kill it.'

'Daddy ordered the cockroach for me,' said Loretta. 'Given how much he paid for Mr Bottomley, it would be very silly if he murdered him two weeks later.'

'And your mother?' asked Fin.

'She's a surgeon,' said Loretta, as if that explained everything.

'So what?' asked April. 'Do you think because she's a medical professional that she's too rational to kill a cockroach?'

'No,' said Loretta. 'I'm saying, if she had any murderous impulses, I'm sure she'd take it out on her human patients first.'

'What was the murder weapon?' asked April, changing the subject.

Fin snorted a laugh. 'You've been playing too much Cluedo. Do you think it was Professor Dumbledore in the conservatory with a candlestick?'

April opened the lid of the small aquarium, peered inside, then sniffed. 'Bug spray.'

Loretta gasped and clutched her chest.

Fin patted her shoulder. He wanted to put his arm around her, but he didn't want her to think he was taking advantage of her grief. 'At least it would have been quick,' he said reassuringly.

'Quick!' exclaimed Loretta. 'Have you ever seen a cockroach killed with bug spray? The poor things flail about for ages. Even after they've collapsed on their backs their little legs flinch and shudder for an eternity.'

'Spraying a cockroach in an aquarium isn't very sporting either,' said April. 'It doesn't have any chance to escape. It's like shooting fish in a barrel, only more sensible because if you actually shot a fish in a barrel, you'd probably shoot a hole in the barrel as well and then you'd get your feet wet.'

'So not only did someone kill my beloved pet and potential champion,' said Loretta, 'they broke into my house to do it!'

'They probably broke into your house while you were out breaking into other people's houses,' said Fin.

Loretta glared at him. 'The fact that it is ironic does not make it any less painful.'

Fin blushed.

'But who would do something so . . . so . . .' said Joe.

'Cruel,' said Loretta.

'No, so . . .' began Joe.

'So vicious?' asked Fin.

'No, I was going to say s-s-so weird,' said Joe.

'A competitor,' said Loretta coldly. 'Cockroach racing is a serious business. Lots of people would want to bump off Mr Bottomley.'

'They might want to, but who'd break into a house to do it?' asked Fin.

'Anyone,' said Loretta. 'This town may seem nice and friendly, but let me tell you, once a year they all go cockroach crazy and lose their minds.'

'You're going to have to narrow down the list of suspects,' said April. 'Is there anyone in particular who might have it in for your cockroach?'

'Well, Matilda Voss-Nevers was very cross with me after last year's race,' said Loretta.

'You know her?' asked Fin.

'Oh yes,' said Loretta. 'We were both in the same heat last year. She was angry because my cockroach was much faster than hers, especially after it bit her cockroach's leg off.'

'She's definitely crazy enough to pull a stunt like this,' said April.

'Anyone else?' asked Fin.

'It could be one of the competitors from last year's final,' said Loretta.

'Why? What happened last year?' asked Fin.

'I didn't break any rules,' said Loretta defensively. 'The accusations of cheating were totally unfair.'

'What did you do?' asked April.

Loretta looked only the tiniest bit shamefaced when she confessed. 'I used a hair dryer.'

'But cockroaches don't have hair,' snapped April. She was confused now, which always made her angry.

'No, but they are highly sensitive to every small disturbance in the air,' explained Loretta. 'That's how they detect approaching threats. So if there is even a tiny movement in the atmosphere, they'll react with lightning-fast reflexes.'

'Hence the hair dryer,' said Fin.

'Yes,' said Loretta. 'You see, it's in the rules that you can't touch your cockroach once the race begins, but there was nothing to say you couldn't blow your cockroach in the rear with a 1000-watt cordless hair dryer.'

'So you won?' said Joe.

'No,' said Loretta sadly. 'People got surprisingly upset. There was a riot. Several cockroaches were lost and the race was abandoned.'

'So that's why everyone in town hates you,' said April. 'Apart from your personality, of course.'

'Yes, I'm afraid people in Currawong don't embrace imagination in sportsmanship,' said Loretta.

'You mean cheating,' said April.

'I prefer to think of it as "competitive innovation",' said Loretta.

April fake coughed. 'Cheating.'

'So Mr Bottomley's killer c-could be anyone in town,' said Joe.

'That's why I need you to help me,' said Loretta, turning to April and Fin with a disarming smile. 'You're new and no one likes you.'

'Hey, how did you know that?' asked Fin.

'Intuition,' said Loretta kindly. 'No one will mind if you ask some questions.'

'Why don't you investigate yourself?' asked April.

'The races are in five days and there are eight thousand suspects,' said Loretta. 'I may be stunningly beautiful and staggeringly intelligent, but even I need help with a problem of this magnitude.'

'We'll help you,' said Fin, in his deep voice again.

'We will?' said April. It was not in her nature to be agreeable.

'It's only neighbourly,' said Fin.

'You've never wanted to be neighbourly before,'

said April. 'When we lived in the city we had elderly neighbours who would have loved help occasionally and you never offered.'

'I've grown as a person,' said Fin.

'You just think she's pretty,' accused April.

'I do not!' said Fin, turning red in the face.

'You don't?' asked Loretta.

'She is pretty,' said Joe. 'That's just objectively true.'

'I know,' said Loretta with a smile.

'Come on, April. Let's help her,' said Fin. 'We need to get involved in some after-school activities, we might as well make cockroach murder investigating one of them. It beats violin lessons.'

Chapter 14

THE INVESTIGATION BEGINS . . . BADLY

The following morning the Peski kids decided to eat breakfast in town. It wasn't a hard decision, because after just twenty-four hours of living with Dad they had eaten all the food in his house. Even the disgusting high-fibre bran cereal was gone. Dad had offered to pick some vegetables, but no child wants to eat salad for breakfast, so Fin had persuaded Dad to give them some money instead, arguing that they should go into town and integrate with the local community while eating bacon and eggs.

The Peski kids stood on the main street of town, considering their dining alternatives.

'There's not a lot of choice, is there?' said Fin.

There was a Chinese restaurant, the type that served food no actual Chinese person would recognise as coming from their country. Chips were included with every meal.

'The Chinese restaurant isn't open yet,' said Joe.

A few shops down there was the other extreme – The Leafy Green Bistro. A vegan fair-trade health food cafe that made its own bread entirely out of lentils.

'I refuse to eat health food,' said April stubbornly.

'*Arf!*' Pumpkin barked his agreement.

This left only one alternative. The Good Times Cafe. The kids stared in through the front window. The cafe looked like it had been decorated in the 1950s and not updated since. Even the windows appeared not to have been cleaned in decades.

'In the city they'd say this place had retro charm,' said Fin.

'Nah,' said April. 'They'd say it's a dump.'

'Yes, but a charming retro dump,' said Fin.

'There's nothing charming about food poisoning,' said April, 'which is what we'll get if they wash their dishes as rarely as they wash these windows.'

'I don't care. They've got five-dollar egg and bacon rolls,' said Joe, pointing to a handwritten sign sticky-taped to the inside of the glass door. 'I'm going in.'

The inside was just as underwhelming as the exterior. All the tables were booths. Most of the vinyl seats had cracks that had been half-heartedly 'fixed' with gaffer tape and the walls were lined with photographs of Currawong one hundred years ago. April peered at one, then another, then turned and looked out at the street.

'Currawong one hundred years ago looks exactly the same as it does now,' said April.

There was absolutely no difference in the street-scape. The fire station, the newsagency, the pub – they all looked exactly the same in the sepia photographs as they did in full colour out on the street.

'There are cars now,' said Fin. He pointed to the vehicles in the street. 'In the photos, it's horse-drawn carts.'

April looked out the window just as a horse-drawn cart drove down the middle of the road. She smiled triumphantly.

'I stand corrected,' said Fin.

They chose a booth after a brief wrestle over who would sit in the seat facing the door, which April won. Pumpkin scrambled up on the seat next to her and they all settled down to look at the menu.

A sulky waitress dressed entirely in black, including black nail polish and lipstick, begrudgingly made her way over to their table. She had earbuds in with music playing so loudly the Peski kids could hear the pounding beat of death metal from where they were sitting. The waitress sighed, took one bud out of her ear and turned her notepad to a new page. Joe noticed that her name tag read *'Hi, my name is Joy.'* He suddenly realised that Joy had been watching him as he stared at her chest. He gulped.

'Well?' said Joy.

'W-w-w-w-w . . .' Joe's stammer always grew worse when he was nervous or someone frightened him.

'We'll have three egg and bacon rolls and three chocolate milkshakes, please,' said Fin.

'I want lime,' said April.

'Lime milkshakes are gross,' said Fin.

'So are you!' said April, slapping the menu shut and kicking him under the table at the same time.

Pumpkin started barking. He had spotted a rat under another table and ran off to chase it.

Joy sighed again then slowly made her way over to the kitchen service hatch to pin up their order.

'Do you think she suffers from chronic fatigue syndrome?' asked Fin.

'I'm sure she does,' said April. 'This awful town would have that effect on anybody.'

'We should start work investigating the mystery of Loretta's dead cockroach,' said Fin.

'Fine,' said April. She pointed to two boys sitting at a booth on the other side of the diner. 'There are two kids over there shoving leaves into a shoebox. You don't have to be Sherlock Holmes to figure out that either they're weirdos with a thing for leaves, or they've got a cockroach in there.'

'That's Animesh and Kieran,' said Fin. He knew this because he'd tried to memorise his classmates' names the day before. 'You remember, Pumpkin tore Kieran's pants yesterday in PE.'

'Whatever,' said April. 'Let's just go and talk to them.'

April slid out of the booth and set off, striding across the diner. Fin hurried to catch up with her as she confronted the two boys.

'What have you got in the box?' demanded April.

'Nothing,' said Animesh, putting his hands protectively on top of the box.

'You're lying,' said April. 'I saw you shoving leaves in there, so at the very least you've got leaves inside.'

'April, maybe you should try being polite,' muttered Fin.

'Ergh,' said April, making a disparaging noise in the back of her throat. 'I'm not good at that, so I'm not going to bother.'

Fin tried instead. 'What my sister means is, sorry to intrude, but have you got a cockroach in there?' asked Fin.

Kieran picked up the shoebox and hugged it to his chest.

'You're new here so you don't understand,' said Kieran. 'People mind their own business when it comes to cockroaches.'

April rolled her eyes. 'The social subtleties of this town are more complicated than the French court under Louis the fourteenth.'

'Huh?' said Animesh.

'It's because we're new that we're asking,' said Fin. 'We've got our own cockroach and we want to know how to prepare it for the race. What should we be feeding it? How should we be training it?'

'You have to spend time with your roach. Get to know it, get to know how it thinks,' said Kieran. He tapped the side of his forehead and squinted as he said this, as if he were really straining to think on the same wavelength as an insect right at that moment.

'I bet you've got a head start on knowing how a cockroach thinks,' said April. 'You've got about as many brain cells.'

'April,' said Fin with a forced smile, 'please, be nice.'

'I am being nice,' protested April. 'I haven't thumped anyone yet, have I?'

'So have you got any tips for us?' asked Fin, smiling at Kieran and Animesh.

'Why are you asking them for tips?' said April. 'We're meant to be asking about Loretta's cockroach.'

'You know Loretta Viswanathan?' asked Animesh, with a look of panic on his face.

'Kind of,' said Fin. 'She's our next-door neighbour.'

Animesh and Kieran leapt to their feet and gathered up their bags. 'You're spying for the enemy!'

'We only met her yesterday,' said April. 'It's not like she's our friend.'

'Yeah, April doesn't have friends,' said Fin. 'She's too horrible.'

April nodded because this was entirely true.

'So she's paying you to spy for her, is she?' demanded Kieran. 'That would be right. Those rich kids over at St Anthony's will stoop to anything.'

━━━━━━

While April and Fin cross-examined Kieran and Animesh, Joe was eating his egg and bacon roll. The waitress may have looked like an extra from a horror movie, but the chef was clearly a maestro. The bacon was crispy and the egg was cooked 'over easy' so the yolk exploded and dripped down his hands as he ate. It was the perfect sandwich. Joe sighed with contentment.

Suddenly, something flicked him on the back of the head. Joe instinctively rubbed the spot, although there was nothing there anymore. Then he looked around. There was a folded-up note lying on the seat behind him. Joe unfolded the note. It read . . .

I think you're dishy. Come with me to the Ball.
♥ Daisy Odinsdottir.

Joe looked up. There was a group of girls sitting in a booth and staring at him. They all giggled and turned away. Except for one girl. She smiled. Joe pointed at her, then at the note with a questioning look on his face as if to say, 'Is this from you?'. She nodded with a smile, blew him a kiss, then turned back to her friends.

Joe went bright red. He was terrified. Was this some sort of practical joke? By 'ball' he assumed she meant a dance. But he couldn't believe that this strange town would actually have one of those. Surely that sort of thing only happened in fairytales and movies. And why on earth would an apparently attractive girl want to go with him? She must be under some sort of misapprehension that he was much more interesting than he was. Perhaps April had been spreading wild rumours that he was a billionaire's grandson, or seventeenth in line to the throne of Borneo. That was the type of thing April would do, thinking it was hysterically funny.

Joe couldn't believe a girl would actually ask him on a date. He had never been on a date before. He had thought about it, but he couldn't see any way of going on a date without speaking, so he had never pursued the idea.

Meanwhile, back on the other side of the diner, April was not letting up on Animesh and Kieran. 'Just show us the cockroach,' demanded April.

'Please,' added Fin. 'We're new here. We're trying to understand your local customs so we can learn how to fit in. I thought people here in Currawong were meant to be friendly.'

Appealing to his Currawongian spirit must have worked, because Kieran relented and carefully lifted the lid. They leaned forward to get a closer look.

'It *is* just a box full of leaves,' said April, rolling her eyes. 'Wow, I didn't see that coming.'

'He's under the leaves, nitwit,' said Kieran scathingly.

Animesh reached in and lifted a clump of leaves. That's when they saw it. A wet brown stain pressed into the cardboard floor of the box. From the flecks of exoskeleton and disembodied legs, this flat brown stain had clearly, until recently, been a living cockroach.

'Nooooo!' cried Animesh, bursting into tears.

'There must be some mistake,' said Kieran. He lifted up the rest of the leaves, but the squashed stain was the only cockroach in the box.

'Look at that,' said April. 'There's a footprint.' Over the top of the squashed stain was the dusty shape of a shoe.

'You!' screamed Animesh. 'You did this!'

'I did not!' protested April. 'That's just stupid. If I was going to kill your cockroach, I wouldn't come over and chat with you afterwards, would I?'

'You crazy city kids will do anything for attention,' accused Animesh.

'It can't have been me,' said April. 'My shoe doesn't match that footprint. Here look . . .' She took off her shoe and held it over the footprint. It was the exact same size.

'That's a precise match!' yelled Animesh.

April looked at the sole of her shoe.

'The tread pattern is the same too!' accused Kieran.

Even April was alarmed. She was racking her memory to think if she had stepped on the cockroach and forgotten about it, but that was impossible.

'It wasn't me,' said April. She sounded unsure, even to herself.

'There must be loads of people with the same shoe size,' said Fin.

'Yeah, but no one else is an outsider,' said Kieran, narrowing his eyes.

'What's that supposed to mean?' asked April.

'I think it means we're outsiders,' said Fin. 'Which is technically true.'

'Outsiders never understand the races,' said Kieran. 'They don't get it. They don't appreciate the honour and the history of the festival.'

'They just think cockroaches are gross and want to stomp on them,' added Animesh.

'Yeah!' said someone else in the diner. Other Currawong residents were starting to mutter and glare.

'If I didn't think I was about to become the victim of physical violence, I would find this situation interesting,' said Fin, looking about. 'This is clearly how lynch mobs get started.'

Joy, the waitress, picked up the wall phone behind the counter and started dialling.

'We are trying to do the right thing here. The only reason we were talking to you in the first place,' said April, now talking to the whole diner, 'was because we're investigating who killed Loretta Viswanathan's cockroach.'

There were gasps and exclamations of shock from customers all around the cafe.

'What?' asked Fin. 'What's the big deal?'

'Loretta Viswanathan,' said Animesh coldly, 'is unsportsmanlike.'

The entire cafe looked very serious and sober about this. Even Joy managed to look more miserable at the mention of Loretta's name.

'Most professional athletes are unsportsmanlike,' said April. 'That's how they get to be so good at sport.'

'You'd better come along with me,' said a man with a gruff voice.

April turned, about to yell at whoever had the temerity to interrupt when she noticed the colour of his shirt. It was blue. She looked up. The owner of the blue shirt also had epaulets, a walkie-talkie and a gun holster. It was a police officer.

'You must be the new kids I've heard so much about,' said the officer. 'I'm Senior Constable Pike and I'm the law in this town.'

Fin failed to suppress a snigger.

'What are you laughing at?' asked Constable Pike.

'You said "I'm the law in this town",' said Fin. 'You sound like a sheriff in a cowboy movie.

Constable Pike scowled. 'We'll talk about this down at the station.'

Joe hurried over. He normally let April and Fin sort out their conflicts with other kids. April got into so many arguments that if he got involved in them all, he would be busy all day. But when an actual official law enforcement officer turns up, he had to step up and be the responsible big brother. 'It's okay, it's j-j-just kid stuff. We'll sort it out.'

'This is not just kid stuff,' said Constable Pike. 'These two individuals have created a disturbance at a public dining establishment.'

April spun around and glared at Joy. 'You snitched?' she accused.

Joy glared sulkily back. 'Ahuh,' she confirmed.

'This town is insane,' said April.

'Come with me, you three,' said Constable Pike, taking a step towards the doorway.

'No,' said Fin. 'You can't make us go to the police station unless you arrest us.'

'That's the way it's going to be, is it?' demanded Constable Pike, getting angry now. 'So you're city kids, all studied up on your legal rights, are you? Been reading lots of fancy law books?'

'No,' said Fin. 'I just watch a lot of cop shows on TV.'

'Fine,' said Constable Pike. 'Then I am arresting you.'

'W-W-What for?' asked Joe, alarmed at how this situation was billowing out of control.

'Swearing at a police officer,' said Constable Pike.

'But we haven't sworn at you,' said Fin.

'Not yet,' muttered April.

Constable Pike thought hard for a moment, then an idea came to him. 'Intimidation!'

Fin looked at April and then at the police officer, who was two feet taller and easily twice her body weight. 'You're intimidated by her?'

Constable Pike appeared to be boiling with rage now. He pressed his lips together and his face turned red. He put his hand on his hips, ready to have a good yell at the Peski kids when suddenly Pumpkin launched into action. Until this point he had been distracted by eating the rat he had killed, but now he noticed that his mistress needed him and he was energised. Pumpkin bounded across the restaurant and sank his teeth into Constable Pike's ankle.

'Aaaaaggghhh!' cried Constable Pike, trying to pull his leg away from Pumpkin. But the dog just took this to be a lovely game, and sunk his teeth in deeper as the police officer waved his leg back and forth in the air. 'That's it. I'm arresting you for keeping a dangerous animal!'

Chapter 15

SERIOUSLY

Ten minutes later, the Peski kids were all assembled at the police station, which was actually a charming sandstone building with beautiful flowerboxes outside every window. There wasn't a lot of crime in Currawong, so Constable Pike spent a fair bit of time gardening. April was handcuffed to her chair. In the end, she really had assaulted the constable when he couldn't take the shin injuries anymore and had locked Pumpkin in a holding cell.

Now the three Peski kids were sitting across from Constable Pike in an interview room. Mr Lang, their guidance counsellor, was also present. He had been called down from the school to stand in as a responsible adult witness. They'd called Dad first but he hadn't answered the phone.

'He's probably in the garden,' said Joe.

'Yeah, fixing all the damage Loretta did with her horse,' said April.

'No, he's probably in the house but not answering the phone because he's paranoid it's bugged,' said Fin, not wanting to think badly of Loretta or her horse.

Mr Lang's presence was probably the only thing stopping Constable Pike from throttling the children. He'd had his worst morning on duty since he'd been transferred to Currawong fourteen years ago, and that included the morning when his squad car had been swept into the creek by floodwaters and he'd ended up floating in Wakagala Dam.

'Why did you do it?' demanded Constable Pike, glaring at April and Fin. 'What sort of sick conspiracy have you cooked up?'

'It's just a cockroach,' said April.

'Just a cockroach!' bellowed Constable Pike

incredulously. 'That could have been a championship winner. But we'll never know now, thanks to you.'

'Constable,' chided Mr Lang.

'Senior Constable,' Constable Pike corrected him.

'Yes, well, I taught you in fifth grade so I'm going to call you what I called you then,' said Mr Lang. 'Bob, you need to tone it down. You can't yell at the children yet. It hasn't been proven.'

'Sorry, sir,' said Constable Pike. 'I'm just so upset.'

'I know,' said Mr Lang. 'We all are.'

'This is like an episode of the *Twilight Zone*,' said Fin. 'We've entered a parallel universe where cockroaches are really important.'

'And dental hygiene isn't,' said April, looking at the constable's teeth.

'It wasn't us who killed the cockroach,' said Fin, speaking slowly and calmly to Constable Pike. 'There was no time before we spoke to Kieran and Animesh.'

'There must have been time,' said Constable Pike. 'The cockroach didn't squash itself.'

'I'd squash myself if I had to spend time with Animesh and Kieran,' said April.

'But perhaps it had already been squashed then,' said Fin, ignoring April. 'We just saw the boys shoving leaves in the box. It could have been squashed before we got to the cafe. Perhaps they squashed it themselves because they knew it wasn't going to win.'

'Ooh, I like that theory,' said April. 'Perhaps one of them did it accidentally, then didn't have the courage to tell the other. I bet it's Kieran. He looks shifty. His eyes are too small for his head.'

'Kieran is my nephew,' said Senior Constable Pike, glowering.

April looked at the police officer. 'Oh yes, I can see the family resemblance now,' said April. 'Your eyes are tiny too.'

'April!' chided Fin. 'Please don't make the nice policeman even angrier.'

'What?' protested April. 'I'm only stating a physical fact.'

'Just because it's true,' said Fin, 'doesn't make it polite.'

'If I worried about being polite, I'd never say anything,' said April.

'I think we'd all prefer that,' said Fin.

'If you confess now,' said Mr Lang, 'and give a detailed account of what you did and how you did it, I'm sure Constable Pike will take that into account and be lenient with you.'

'What?' said Constable Pike. 'I will not!'

'They're not going to confess if you threaten to lock them up and throw away the key,' said Mr Lang.

'I can't do that anyway,' grumbled Constable Pike. 'The magistrate over in Bilgong never takes cockroach-related crime seriously.'

'Apparently the Viswanathan girl's cockroach has been killed too,' said Mr Lang.

'No way!' said Constable Pike. 'That makes six this week.'

'Six what?' asked Joe.

'He's not talking about days, is he?' asked April. 'He does realise there are seven days in a week.'

'The sixth cockroach that's been nobbled,' said Constable Pike. 'Cindy Wu's roach was found dead two days ago, old man McGregor's roach fell into a paper shredder and Wilhelmina Dibbet's whole stable of roaches was wiped out when someone put a glue trap in their enclosure.'

'That's half the town's top roaches,' said Mr Lang, shaking his head at the magnitude of the crime spree.

'I know,' said Constable Pike gravely.

'Can't people just catch some more?' asked April.

Constable Pike bristled. 'These people are grieving for their loved ones. How dare you suggest something so insensitive?'

'Can we go now?' asked Fin. 'We didn't do anything.'

Constable Pike scoffed. 'Huh, I don't believe that for a second.'

'You've got no evidence,' said April. 'You can't arrest us.'

'Apart from anything else, killing cockroaches isn't a crime,' said Fin.

'Actually, it is in Currawong,' said Mr Lang. 'Injuring another person's cockroach is punishable with a $2000 fine.'

'We should get their parents down here,' said Constable Pike. 'If we can't throw the book at the kids, perhaps they'll punish them appropriately.'

'Our mother is mi–' began April.

'Overseas on a w-w-work trip,' Joe interrupted.

'Get their dad in then,' said Constable Pike.

'We can't,' said Mr Lang with a sigh. 'Mr Peski has a note from his doctor excusing him from all parent meetings.'

'Can a parent even do that?' asked Constable Pike.

'Apparently,' said Mr Lang.

'Well, if I see either of you kids acting suspiciously, I'll arrest you faster than you can say "habeas corpus",' said Constable Pike menacingly.

'Can we report you for threatening innocent children?' asked April.

'I'm a cop in a small town,' said Constable Pike. 'It's my job to threaten and intimidate children.'

Chapter 16

AT HOME

Dad was not in the garden. And he was not hiding from imaginary assassins. When Constable Pike had tried calling him, Dad did not answer the phone because he was busy. The electronic bug detector he had ordered on the internet had arrived in the post, and he was putting it to use. Dad was on his hands and knees under the desk in his office running the detector along the wall. It lit up like a department store on Christmas Eve. There was definitely an electromagnetic signal coming from the spot that corresponded with the drill hole on the outside of the house. There was only one way to figure out what it was. Dad picked up the chainsaw he had also ordered on the internet and pulled the starter cord. The chainsaw screamed to life. *Brrap-rraap-rappp-RRAAAP!* Dad stepped forward and started to hack a hole in the dry wall.

Thirty seconds later, he was holding a tiny electronic device in his hand. It was the size of a medicine capsule, but the scanner clearly showed it was emitting a CDMA signal. The type the military use to send information.

Dad dabbed his forehead with his handkerchief. He didn't know what to do. Someone was listening to him, here in his own home. He'd been found.

Dad got to his feet and set the scanner on his bookcase. He should call Professor Maynard, but he had no contact details for her. Just then, the scanner's LED display lit up again. Dad picked the scanner up and ran it along the bookshelf. All the bars flashed. There was an electromagnetic device there as well. Dad tried the window frame. The scanner lit up again. Then the door. Another device. He kept searching, methodically making his way through the house.

By the time he had finished with the scanner and the chainsaw there was a pile of 136 tiny electronic emitters sitting in a bowl on his kitchen table. They were all different sizes and shapes. Some were tiny capsule devices, others were larger boxes with pinhole cameras. Dad sat on a stool, trembling. He didn't know what to do. He was overwhelmed with a feeling of terrible dread. He had to do something. But what? And how could he do something when he couldn't stop shaking. Eventually Dad dug deep and found the courage to stand up. He picked up the bowl full of electronic bugs and tipped them into the blender. After three minutes on the pulse setting there were no more electronic signals being emitted.

All three Peski kids were dejected as they trudged up their driveway that afternoon. The second day of school had gone even worse than the first. Word had soon spread about the debacle at the Good Times Cafe. No one had spoken to April or Fin all day. Joe, on the other hand, had the opposite problem.

Now that he had the reputation of a lawn bowls master, girls had been following him around, staring at him with moony eyes and giggling.

'What did you do?' April asked Joe.

'Huh?' said Joe.

'At lunchtime I was cornered by a group of year 10 girls demanding to know where you were,' explained April.

'Did you tell one of them they were fat?' asked Fin. 'Girls hate that.'

'Everyone hates that,' said April.

'Sumo wrestlers don't,' said Fin.

'Okay, everyone except sumo wrestlers,' said April. 'And I haven't noticed any female sumo wrestlers enrolled at Currawong High School.'

'Maybe they don't go out much because they're sensitive to the sun,' said Fin.

'So you're saying there's a pasty-pale female sumo wrestler hidden somewhere in the school and Joe has gone out of his way to insult her?' asked April.

'Well, we all know Joe isn't very good at making conversation,' said Fin.

'Shut up,' said Joe.

'Point proven,' said Fin.

Joe shoved Fin. He didn't push him hard, but Fin was in the middle of taking a step so it was enough to make him overbalance into a grevillea bush.

'Hey!' said Fin.

'He told you to shut up,' smirked April.

Fin scrambled after them.

'Thank goodness you're here!' cried Dad, bursting out of the front door. He looked frazzled. His hair was uncombed, which was actually pretty standard for Dad. But his jumper was inside out and he was wearing mismatched shoes, so he looked even more stressed than usual. Pumpkin barked excitedly and rushed forward. He loved biting Dad.

'What's the problem?' asked April. 'Have you been attacked by a pasty female sumo wrestler too?'

'The Japanese are after us as well?!' exclaimed Dad. 'All the more reason to make haste. Quick children, grab your bags. We're going!' Dad ducked back into the house and returned a second later with four suitcases. He threw one each to the children.

'Going where?' asked Joe.

'I'm not going to tell you,' said Dad, as he tried to wrestle Pumpkin away from his trouser cuff. 'If you don't know they can't torture it out of you. Come on.'

Dad picked up his own bag and started hurrying round the side of the house. The children looked at each other.

'What's got into him?' asked Fin.

'Who knows,' said April. 'Too much exposure to cockroach spray probably.'

'Better follow him,' said Joe, walking off in the direction Dad had disappeared.

As they turned round the side of the house, they could see Dad at the far end of the garden making his way towards the big garden shed.

'He's not going to make us do gardening, is he?' asked Fin. 'I didn't sign up for that.'

As they drew nearer they could hear Dad rattling about on the other side of the shed's big double doors.

'What's he doing?' asked April.

Just then the bolt lock slid open and both doors swung out, revealing a state-of-the-art helicopter.

'Wow!' said Joe

'Hop in,' said Dad.

'Wait a second,' said April. 'Do you even know how to fly this?'

'Of course,' said Dad. 'I am a graduate from a top Samoan online flying academy.'

'Online?' said Fin. 'But have you flown an actual helicopter before?'

'I've flown hundreds of hours on the simulator,' said Dad. 'I know what I'm doing.' He kicked out the chocks from in front of the wheels.

'Where d-d-did you g-get it?' asked Joe. He didn't know much about helicopters but he imagined they were very expensive.

'I built it,' said Dad. 'You can get kits online. It's just an internal combustion engine attached to a rotor and an anti-torque rotor. It wasn't hard.'

'But where are we going?' asked April.

Dad looked about nervously. 'I can't tell you,' he said. 'The walls have ears.'

'This is ridiculous,' said April, turning on her heel and heading back towards the house. 'I'm going to get a snack.'

'Come back!' cried Dad. 'Our lives are in danger.'

'Too right,' April called over her shoulder. 'We're doomed if we get in that death-trap with you.'

'Sorry, Dad,' said Fin, slapping his father on the shoulder. 'I'm sure when I get to know you better I'll love you like a . . . well, like a father. But even then, I'm not getting in that thing with you.'

Fin followed April back towards the house. Leaving only Joe with Dad.

'But we're in terrible danger here,' said Dad, pleading with Joe. He leaned forward and whispered. 'I found bugs in the house.'

Joe didn't know how to respond.

'Hundreds of them,' whispered Dad, checking over his shoulder in case one of the bushes was listening in.

'But I thought you had the h-h-house sprayed for that?' said Joe.

Now Dad was confused. 'No, the other type of bugs,' he said, realising what Joe meant. 'The listening ones.'

'Right,' said Joe, thinking his Dad was barmy but not liking to say so to his face. 'I'm sure you're right, but this h-h-helicopter thing is too c-c-crazy. I think we'd rather take our chances with the bugs, the crawly ones and the listening ones. Sorry.'

Joe started walking back to the house too.

Dad hesitated. Every fibre of his body was screaming at him to jump in the helicopter and get out of there. But deep down in his soul, another voice was talking to him too. A voice telling him that he must not abandon his kids.

Dad started to shake. He was so frightened. But he couldn't do it. He couldn't leave his children. True, he'd only just met them. And he didn't particularly like them yet. But they looked like their mother, and he had loved their mother dearly. So now he felt something he had never felt before. The instinct to protect. It was the same way he felt when he saw newly hatched ducklings. He felt teary and emotional.

Dad slumped. He was going to have to be brave. He hated being brave. He swung the doors shut and re-bolted the shed, then headed back across the garden. Perhaps one of the children would make him a snack too.

Chapter 17

FRAMED AGAIN

Joe, Fin and April paused before they entered the school gates. Pumpkin stopped to chew on the sign that said 'No dogs on school premises'.

'Well, today can't be as bad as yesterday,' said Fin philosophically.

'Of course it can, nitwit,' said April. 'Yesterday was bad, but none of us suffered irreparable brain injuries or had our legs eaten off by crocodiles.'

'I'd rather suffer a brain injury than have to face D-Daisy again,' said Joe.

'Is she ugly?' asked Fin.

'Worse,' said Joe. 'Incredibly good-looking. She's absolutely t-terrifying.'

'Do you want me to wrestle her for you?' asked April.

Joe did consider this for a second. 'B-Better not,' he decided. 'She might like it.' Joe pushed opened the gate and headed off towards the senior playground.

Fin and April reluctantly made their way to the junior area. As they crossed the playground there were no words of abuse or sneering comments. They were met with eerie silence. All conversation stopped as they approached. People glared and moved away as if they were diseased. It was only fifty metres to the verandah where they had to drop their bags, but the walk seemed to take forever.

'What are *you* looking at?' April snapped at a small girl who hadn't moved away quick enough. The girl didn't respond, except to scurry off.

'It only took two days to become the most unpopular kids in school,' said Fin.

'Pfft,' said April. 'They'll come round. I've got a cute and adorable puppy.'

At that moment, Pumpkin was going to the toilet on someone's backpack. Fin loathed his sister in so many ways, but he had to admire her blind stubbornness and determination.

'Anyway, who wants to be friends with these weirdos?' said April.

Fin watched the rest of the kids in the playground. 'I think by any objective measure, we are the weirdos in this scenario.'

'You are,' agreed April. 'But I'm the coolest kid in this school. They're just too dumb to know it.'

'Okay,' said Fin. Sometimes it was easier not to argue, especially if you didn't want a black eye before first period.

The bell rang. Matilda ran over and swept up her bag. It had been near Fin's feet. 'You stay away from my roach,' said Matilda, clutching her bag to her chest.

'I didn't do anything,' argued Fin.

'Yeah right,' said Matilda. 'Everyone's knows what happened at the cafe.'

'Really? We don't know and we were there,' said April.

'Just stay away,' said Matilda, slinging her backpack up onto her shoulder. 'Hey, why is my bag wet?'

'Good dog, Pumpkin,' said April. He sat proudly at her feet while she gave him a pat. 'Maybe I *will* kill some cockroaches today,' muttered April. 'Just to show these country kids a thing or two.'

Fin grabbed April by the forearm. 'Don't, please don't. We have to live here. There are no other schools we can get transferred to.'

'Come in,' said Miss Hickson, their art teacher. April relaxed. She liked art. Fin suspected there was some therapeutic value for her. Like basket weaving, it pacified her.

'We're going to be doing abstract expressionism today,' said Miss Hickson happily.

Every student had a square metre of canvas and five litres of paint in each of the primary colours, plus black and white.

'But what do you want us to paint?' asked Fin.

'Your emotions,' said Miss Hickson.

'An emotion isn't a thing,' said Fin. 'You can't paint it.'

'I want you to express your feelings,' said Miss Hickson.

'But what if I don't have feelings,' said Fin, 'or they're so repressed I don't know what they are.'

Feelings were not Fin's greatest strength. He could do fear, stress and irritation, but the more subtle gradations in between were beyond him.

'Just paint that then,' said Miss Hickson, beginning to get peevish.

Fin looked around. April was already squirting big dollops of paint on her canvas. She had a manic but uncharacteristically joyful expression on her face. The rest of the class seemed to be getting in the spirit too. There were squeals of delight and giggles as paint went everywhere.

Fin sighed. He didn't care what Miss Hickson said. He was not going to express his emotions. He didn't want to. If he used the paint to make as much mess as possible, he was sure she wouldn't be able to tell the difference.

The double lesson passed quickly. The painting only took half an hour, but cleaning up after the painting filled the rest of the time and somehow made the students messier. The sinks were outside the classroom and if you cram thirty teenagers around a trough full of water, it is almost impossible to avoid a water fight. Especially when there is so much cockroach-related tension in the air.

It started when someone 'accidentally' tipped a bucket of dirty water all over April, then escalated when she threw a dozen filthy paintbrushes back. Unfortunately, she missed the person who doused her and got seven innocent bystanders. Then it was on. The whole class was grabbing every nearby receptacle and hurling as much water as possible through the air. To start with April was the target of most of it. But as more water went astray, more side battles were created until everyone was just trying to get everyone else wet.

'Enough!' bellowed Miss Hickson.

Everyone froze mid-water fight, suddenly conscious of what they had done. They were all drenched and the art equipment was strewn everywhere. Several water jugs had ended up on the roof and paintbrushes were caught up in a nearby tree. Pumpkin was now largely blue.

There was a dreadful pause as they waited, wondering what Miss Hickson was going to scream at them. But she did something much more shocking. She broke into an enormous smile.

'Well done, everyone,' Miss Hickson beamed. 'You've truly embraced the anarchic spirit of expressionist art. I'm very proud.'

The class collectively unclenched. There was a sense of dizzying euphoria, like you only get when you know you've got away with something you really shouldn't have.

'Now if you'll just clean up the mess you've made cleaning up,' said Miss Hickson, 'you should finish in time for the bell.'

The class hastily sorted out the mess, actually working well as a team to hoist the smallest member of the class, which happened to be Fin, up onto the roof to get down the containers. They knocked the paintbrushes out of the tree with some handy good-sized rocks and were soon finished. Things didn't exactly look tidy, but nor could you tell there had been a near disaster level of mess fifteen minutes earlier.

'Well done. Class dismissed,' said Miss Hickson, as the hooter sounded.

The class started picking up their bags and chattering among themselves.

'You see,' said April defiantly. 'I told you today was going to be better.'

Fin smiled. He had actually enjoyed art. That was practically a miracle. Perhaps April was right.

Suddenly, there was a bloodcurdling scream.

'Aaaaagggghhhh!'

April leapt up onto the desk. 'What is it? A snake? A time bomb?'

'My roach,' wailed Matilda. 'My roach!'

Matilda was holding a chocolate box with the lid open, but the look on her face was a thousand times worse than the look of someone who's just discovered that the only chocolates left were Turkish delight.

'What's she going on about?' asked April.

'I don't think she had chocolates in that box,' said Fin.

People were gathering round Matilda to look.

'It was you!' accused Matilda, pointing at April. 'You did this. You said you would.'

'Do what?' asked April in exasperation.

Matilda turned the box around to show her. 'This!'

April and Fin saw Matilda's roach. It was floating on top of a pool of what looked like bright red blood.

'How can a cockroach bleed that much?' asked April.

'That's not blood,' said Fin. 'It's paint.'

'You drowned Bertha in paint,' accused Matilda.

'I did not!' cried April.

'Look,' said Animesh, pointing at April's painting. 'She didn't use red paint in her picture.'

'Exactly,' said Matilda. 'She couldn't. She was hoarding it all to drown my Bertha.'

'But I never had a chance,' protested April. 'The class has been together the whole time.'

'You could have snuck back in while we were having the water fight,' said Matilda. 'No one would have noticed.'

'Miss Hickson would have noticed,' argued April.

'Actually, I wouldn't,' said Miss Hickson. 'While you were outside enjoying yourselves, I was brewing up a nice cup of tea. I find I always need a nice cup of tea by the end of year 8 art.'

'But I didn't do it!' wailed April.

'You said you were going to kill our cockroaches,' said Matilda. 'I heard you right before art.'

'But she didn't mean it,' said Fin.

'Yes, I did,' said April. 'These kids are really ticking me off. I meant it all right, but I didn't do it. I was too busy.'

'I'm telling Mr Lang,' said Matilda.

'Tattletale,' sneered April.

'Murderer!' accused Matilda.

'Wait!' cried Fin, looking at the cockroach in the box. 'I just saw Bertha move.'

'Aaagghh!' wailed Matilda. 'She's dying slowly. My poor, poor baby.'

'I'll step on her if you'd like, to speed things up,' offered April.

Matilda lunged for April, which was a mistake. April had been waiting for a chance to use some of her judo moves. The two girls wrestled about under the tables, noisily banging into the chairs. Pumpkin joined in, yapping and snapping at Matilda's skirt, trying to get a good grip. The class was loudly cheering Matilda on, so no one noticed at first when Fin scooped up Bertha with his bare hand.

'Now Fin's attacking Bertha!' Animesh yelled over the ruckus.

'No, I'm not,' said Fin, hurrying towards Miss Hickson's desk. 'I'm trying to save her. It's not too late.'

Miss Hickson had a single washbasin. Fin turned the tap on to a gentle pressure and held the roach underneath the stream of water, rinsing the red paint away. Then he turned her over and rinsed her underside.

The room fell silent as they watched Fin work. He grabbed a biro, broke off the end with his teeth and pulled out the ink tube. He used the pen's plastic shell as a pipette to flush water over the roach's delicate antennae until they were also entirely clean. Then he took off his ugly school hat, laid it on the desk and gently placed the roach on top. It didn't move.

'She's dead!' wailed Matilda. 'What am I going to do? I'll never find another roach that good in time.'

'Hush up,' said Fin. He started to blow gently on the roach. Its antennae and wings quivered a little in the breeze. He blew gently again and again.

Suddenly, a leg twitched.

'I don't believe it,' cried Animesh. 'He's doing CPR on a roach and it's working!'

Fin kept blowing. The water was slowly drying off the cockroach. A second later, its antennae quivered and it scurried forward a couple of steps. Two more breaths and the roach scurried right off the cap and tried to hide in Miss Hickson's pencil case.

'It's a miracle,' breathed Matilda.

'You should say "thank you",' said April.

'I wouldn't have to thank anyone if you hadn't tried to kill her in the first place,' shouted Matilda.

'It wasn't me!' cried April.

'Okay, that's enough,' said Miss Hickson. 'The cockroach is fine. I'll find a clean box you can put her in, Matilda.'

But as Miss Hickson turned away and the rest of the class started to gather their things, there was a bloodcurdling scream.

'Aaaaagghhh!' cried Matilda. She was as white as a sheet and there was a horrified look on her face.

Pumpkin was standing on top of the table, chewing something.

'That dog is eating my cockroach!' accused Matilda.

'How do you know?' said April.

'He jumped onto the table and snapped her up!' said Matilda, shuddering at the horror of it all. 'I saw him do it!'

'You've got no proof,' yelled April.

Unfortunately, at that moment Pumpkin stopped chewing, swallowed, burped, and a cockroach leg fell out of his mouth. Pumpkin sat proudly on the desk expecting everyone to be impressed by what he had done.

'Oh dear,' said Fin.

'Waaaagggghhhh!' said Matilda, as she dissolved into hysterical weeping.

'Fin, April, you had better go and see Mr Lang,' ordered Miss Hickson. 'And take that dog with you.'

Chapter 18

CONFRONTATION WITH A BEAUTY

Joe had never been so scared in his life. Daisy had cornered him in the boys' bathroom. He had thought he was safe there. The smell alone should have been enough to put off any normal girl. But Daisy was clearly not normal. She stationed two friends on the door to keep watch and went in after him.

'Are you trying to avoid me?' she asked. Joe's back was pressed to the wall. Daisy had her hands up either side of his shoulders and was leaning in so her face was uncomfortably close to his chest. She would have preferred for her face to be uncomfortably close to his face, to encourage impromptu kissing, but she wasn't tall enough.

Joe had sprinted to the boys' toilets as soon as the bell rang for recess. He had been in there for the full twenty minutes, so clearly he was either avoiding her or he had a terrible bowel problem. Apparently Daisy was not to be deterred by either alternative.

'Er . . .' said Joe, struggling to know what to say. It would have been rude to yell 'GO AWAY!' and he didn't want to hurt Daisy's feelings. He briefly considered yelling 'HELP! I'M BEING ATTACKED!' but he suspected that would be something he could never live down.

'So are you going to ask me to the ball?' asked Daisy. 'The Cockroach Races Ball is a seriously big deal. It's the third most important event in the Currawong Social Calendar. I need to know what colour corsage you'll be buying me so I can match it with my dress.'

'Um . . .' said Joe. His brain was screaming 'I DON'T WANT TO TAKE YOU. I DON'T WANT TO TAKE YOU!' and his mouth was opening and closing, but he couldn't get his vocal cords to make sound. If only Daisy had been able to lip read.

'Obviously, the decision is yours,' she said. 'But pink really suits me. If you tell Maria in the florist it's me you're buying for, she knows the shade of rose I like.'

'N-n-n . . .' said Joe.

'What was that?' asked Daisy, showing the first sign of interest in what Joe might have to say.

'N-No,' said Joe.

'No, what?' asked Daisy. 'No, you don't like pink? I suppose white would do if you have strong feelings about it.'

'N-N-No, I can't take you,' said Joe. Getting out the words was a great strain, but now that he'd finally said them an enormous sense of relief washed over him.

'What?' said Daisy. Apparently just as Joe's vocal cords had started working, Daisy's brain had stopped.

'I can't take you to the b-b-ball,' said Joe, with growing confidence.

'Why not?' asked Daisy.

Joe stared at her. What reason could he give? He couldn't say 'because you terrify me,' or 'because all girls terrify me'. It would be the truth, but it wouldn't be good for his image. And he couldn't say 'because I can barely speak to girls let alone dance with them', because she would probably find that endearing and just use the fact to bully him more. He needed a really good, solid excuse that would make this beautiful girl leave him alone and stop scaring him.

'B-B-Because . . .' began Joe, making the mistake of starting to talk before he knew what he was going to say.

'Because what?' asked Daisy. She was starting to get testy now, and Joe knew that girls like Daisy went from flirty to nasty in a microsecond.

'B-Because . . . er . . .' said Joe, his brain flailing for inspiration, 'I'm taking someone else.' He didn't know where the words came from. Let alone why he said them out loud. He was horrified with himself.

'Someone else?' asked Daisy, her face screwing up unattractively as though this was a deeply distasteful thought. 'Who?'

Joe's brain blanked. He'd only been living in Currawong for three days. He hadn't learned any of the girls' names at school yet. They were all the same to him. Giggly and terrifying. He couldn't tell you what any of them looked like, because he tried not to look girls directly in the face. It was like looking directly at the sun – so dazzling you could do yourself damage. So Joe blurted out the name of the only girl in Currawong he knew: 'Loretta Viswanathan!'

Daisy recoiled as if she'd been slapped.

'You're taking *her*?!' Daisy clearly knew who Loretta was. She was reacting with the body language of someone who had just found out that Joe had smallpox. She shrank back from him as if he were diseased.

'Yes,' said Joe, relieved that Daisy had taken a step back.

'*You're* taking Loretta Viswanathan to the Cock-roach Races Ball?' asked Daisy, her nose wrinkling as though this thought was more disgusting to her than the actual smell of the boys' bathroom.

'Yes,' said Joe.

'Why?' asked Daisy.

This seemed an odd question. While Daisy was the most beautiful girl at Currawong High, Loretta was in another league of beauty. She was as beautiful as a model. And not the type you see in Kmart catalogues. Loretta resembled the type of model you'd see on a Milan catwalk, looking incredibly bored to be wearing the latest impossibly overpriced designer outfit.

'Um . . .' said Joe. Lying was one thing, but fabricating a whole backstory was more than his imagination could handle. He decided to go with the truth. 'Because she's my next-door neighbour.'

'So she got to you first,' said Daisy. 'Typical. Well, don't come crying to me when she rips out your heart and minces it in a meat grinder.'

'Okay,' said Joe. Daisy was frightening him more, not less now. He was glad he had decided to lie. It seemed like a very good decision.

'You know she cheats,' flung out Daisy.

'On boys?' asked Joe, confused by this turn in the conversation.

'No, in the cockroach races,' said Daisy.

'I don't really care,' Joe replied honestly.

Daisy gasped, which was a mistake. You should never inhale sharply in such a smelly room. 'Then you two deserve each other.' With that, she turned on her heel and stormed out.

Joe slumped back against the wall. He had finally got rid of Daisy. It was as if a weight had been lifted off him.

Suddenly, Daisy burst back into the bathroom. Joe hastily stood up straight. 'Scott Benito just asked me to the Cockroach Races Ball and I said yes.'

'He asked you in the five seconds you were gone?' asked Joe incredulously.

'Yes, that's how popular I am,' said Daisy. 'So we'll see you and Loretta at the ball. I look forward to watching how miserable she makes you.'

Daisy stalked off again.

Then Joe had a horrible dawning realisation. He wasn't off the hook at all. Now he had to do something much, much worse. Now he had to ask Loretta Viswanathan to be his date. He considered fainting but he couldn't even do that. The boys' bathroom is no place to collapse.

Chapter 19

SOMETHING IN THE GARDEN

Dad was in the garden gardening. Digging up weeds, pruning and planting were the only things that could calm his never-ending sense of dread. Fear had draped over him like a heavy cloak, weighing him down every second of the day for the past eleven years. Ever since that terrible night when he saw the one woman he truly loved smash in a grown man's nose with a dinner plate. He could barely remember what it had felt like before, when his life was normal. He was so used to his hands shaking, his breath shortening and sweat pouring off him. He lived every day in a constant state of fear that you would normally only experience if you were being chased by a grizzly bear.

But in the last few days it had got worse. Now Dad wasn't just scared for himself, he was scared for his children too. He was terrified of his wife, but at least she'd had the skills to take care of their children. What chance did they have now that he was their last line of defence?

That's why Dad was out in the garden weeding the daisies. Kneeling in the sun, methodically improving the flowerbed, a small section at a time, was the closest he came to meditation. Actual meditation always made him self-conscious. Every time he closed his eyes he was worried that an assassin would leap out and attack him.

Dad had been working his way up the border for over an hour and his body was finally starting to relax. His hands didn't shake so much anymore that he'd accidentally pull up the daisies, and he could go an entire ten minutes without needing the bathroom. This was as close to feeling good as Dad got.

He was able to enjoy the rustle of the wind through the trees, the buzz of the bees collecting nectar from the jasmine plant nearby and the soft bubble of the fountain in his ornamental goldfish pond.

Until he heard it. A sort of *swoosh-thud*. The distinctive sound of a spade cutting into soil.

Dad's first instinct was to play dead. But then he realised it would be suspicious if he was dead in the middle of the garden. He cautiously raised his head so he could look over the French lavender bush in the direction he'd heard the noise come from. He didn't see anything at first, but then he spotted it. Right in the middle of the rhododendron there was a big round bottom. Someone had their head stuck in the bush. Dad could not imagine what they might be doing – planting a listening device, or a booby trap, or a bomb? His brain told him to run away, but then he thought of his children. He couldn't keep letting them down. He was the grown-up. If there was someone dangerous in the garden, he had to confront them.

Dad raised his trowel and started slowly and silently to make his way towards the bottom. He had started shaking again. If James Bond put a cocktail shaker in his hands, he would have had a perfect martini, shaken not stirred.

The bottom quivered as Dad approached it. The intruder was clearly doing something energetic with the front half of their body. Dad had to put a stop to it. He knew he would never really have the courage to hit someone with a trowel, so he threw that down on the grass and ran at the intruder instead. He might not be physically fit or capable, but he was slightly podgy, and the sheer enormity of his bulk ought to do some damage. He hurled himself through the air at the bottom and crash-tackled the intruder headfirst into the bushes.

'Aaaggghh!' screamed the intruder.

'Ow!' wailed Dad, as whoever it was punched him in the face.

'*Vad gör du!*'

They both struggled to their feet and Dad finally got to see the identity of his assailant. She was tall, beautiful and blonde.

'Ingrid?' asked Dad. Ingrid had lived next door for nearly two years, but Dad still couldn't be entirely sure this was her because he never made eye contact with attractive women if he could at all avoid it. He didn't make eye contact with unattractive women either, but he was particularly afraid of attractive ones. That's probably where Joe got it from.

Ingrid was holding a shovel and breathing heavily. She looked a little dishevelled from being thrust head-first into a shrub, but that only enhanced her terrifying Nordic athleticism.

'*Ja*,' said Ingrid, which even Dad could interpret was 'yes'.

'What are you doing in my garden?' he asked. 'I know Loretta likes to come over and wreck things but really, I don't think it's fair for you to do the same as well.'

Ingrid stared at Dad for a long moment. She seemed to be trying to make a decision. Dad hoped it wasn't to hit him over the head with the shovel. Then he had a nasty thought. 'Y-You're not . . . Kolektiv, are you?' He actually whimpered at the idea. 'What am I asking you for?' he added, more talking to himself. 'You only speak Swedish. If you are Kolektiv, I should just run.' He took a step backwards.

Ingrid sighed and dropped the shovel. 'It's okay,' she said, holding up her hands in a non-threatening gesture. 'I just needed to hide something. I'm sorry. I couldn't let her find it. I thought it would be better to hide it over here.'

'You speak English!' exclaimed Dad.

Ingrid rolled her eyes. 'Everyone in Sweden speaks English.'

'Then why did you let everyone believe that you can't?' asked Dad.

'People in this country talk too much,' said Ingrid. 'If they think I can't speak English, they leave me alone.'

Dad could relate to that. It was a clever idea. He was fluent in several Papua New Guinean dialects. Perhaps he could pretend that was all he spoke. He looked over to his now partially crushed rhododendron bush. A blue shape caught his eye.

'Is that what you were hiding?' he asked.

Ingrid actually blushed. Given that her hair was so blonde it was almost white, her now beetroot-red face stood out in contrast.

Dad tilted his head so he could see the blue shape better. 'Is that a can of . . . bug spray?' He smiled. Dad loved bug spray.

Now Ingrid looked ashamed. 'Please don't tell Loretta. I reacted instinctively. I couldn't bear being in the house with that revolting creature.'

'You sprayed Loretta?' asked Dad. Now he was just getting confused.

'No, I sprayed her cockroach,' said Ingrid. 'It was huge and so disgusting. I couldn't sleep at night knowing it was in the next room.'

Dad's face lit up. 'I know exactly how you feel! I hate cockroaches too.'

'You do?' said Ingrid, so relieved to find a kindred spirit.

'They're horrific disease-carrying Jurassic mini-monsters,' said Dad.

'I know!' agreed Ingrid. 'But Dr Viswanathan paid a fortune for it, and Loretta loved it. I'll lose my job if they find out.'

Dad's face fell. He looked at the can. 'Then we'll have to dig a deeper hole. You don't want Vladimir kicking it up when Loretta is show jumping in my garden. I've got a post hole digger. We can put it three feet down and she'll never find it.'

'Thank you!' exclaimed Ingrid. 'Thank you, so much! You won't tell anyone I can speak English, will you?'

'I wouldn't dream of it,' said Dad.

The two of them set to work, as thick as thieves. Dad's hands had stopped shaking again. It always made him feel better to be at work in the garden.

Chapter 20

TALKING TO GIRLS

Joe was dejected when he came home from school. He found Fin and April upstairs going through the junk in Fin's bedroom.

'What happened?' he asked. 'I waited to walk home with you, but some girl called M-M-Matilda was all snide about how you'd g-g-gone home already.'

'We've been banned from attending the cockroach races,' said April angrily. 'And the stupid ball.'

'Can they do that?' asked Joe.

'Apparently the local council has extraordinary powers to introduce regulations in a special space during an emergency situation,' said Fin. 'They actually showed us the text in the town's constitution.'

'B-But what's the emergency?' asked Joe.

'Everyone in town having severe mental health problems,' grumbled April.

'Pumpkin ate Matilda's cockroach. Everyone thinks we're serial cockroach killers,' explained Fin. 'Then April got into an argument with Mr Lang about it all, so she sent herself home from school early.'

'You can't do that,' said Joe. 'You'll get an unexplained absence on your permanent record.'

'I doubt the unexplained absences are going to be the most shocking things on April's permanent record,' said Fin, still going through boxes.

'What are you doing now?' asked Joe. April and Fin looked like they were searching for something.

'Looking for things we can make into a disguise,' said April, tossing aside some old clothes.

'Why?' asked Joe.

'We're not telling you,' said April. 'You're such a good boy now you'd probably dob us in.'

Joe frowned. He had hoped that being a girl, April would be able to help him talk to Loretta. Perhaps even talk to Loretta for him. But since she was being miserable and rude he didn't feel like asking her. Maybe his father would have advice. After all, Dad had married their mother, so he must have spoken to her at some point to make that happen.

Joe trudged back downstairs in search of Dad. He found him in the kitchen washing dirt off his hands.

'Hi, Dad,' said Joe.

'What is it?' asked Dad, flinching. 'I was just garden-ing. That's why my hands are dirty. Nothing else.'

'Okay,' said Joe. 'I was wondering if you could help me.'

'I'm not very good with life-threatening situations that require immediate physical action,' said Dad.

'I know, but it's nothing like that,' said Joe. 'I need to talk to a g-g-girl.'

'Good gracious,' said Dad. 'That's even worse.'

'It is?' asked Joe.

'Oh yes, just don't do it,' urged Dad. 'They're nothing but trouble.'

'But you talked to Mum,' said Joe, 'when you first met her, d-d-didn't you?'

'Yes,' agreed Dad. 'I don't know how I found the courage. In hindsight, I wonder if she was using one of her super-spy mind-altering rays on me at the time.'

'I wish someone would use a m-m-mind-altering ray on me,' said Joe.

'You could always write a letter,' suggested Dad. 'It's much easier, because you don't have to look at the girl while you're thinking up the words.'

'Nah,' said Joe. 'Quicker to just get the humiliation over with.'

Joe headed out. He would rather drill a hole in his own foot than talk to Loretta, but it had to be done. The talking, not the drilling. At least he didn't have far to walk. Joe only made it halfway down the driveway when he heard a clatter of hooves and looked up to see a big brown stallion galloping towards him.

'Aaagghh!' cried Joe as he leapt out of the way, diving into a bush.

The horse pulled up, skidding a little on the gravel, then reared up in protest. Loretta sat forward in her seat as her horse stomped down, snorting and huffing dramatically.

'Oh stop being so silly, Vlad,' Loretta chided her

horse. 'It's only a boy.' She called out to Joe. 'Are you all right?'

'Y-Y-Yes,' lied Joe. He had landed in a rose bush and had several thorns imbedded in his palms, but he hadn't been kicked in the head by a horse so he considered himself lucky.

'We didn't expect to see you there, did we, Vlad?' said Loretta, patting her horse before looking up at Joe. 'You know, it would be much safer if you walked across the lawn.'

'This is our driveway,' said Joe.

'Yes, but Daddy doesn't like it when I gallop on our own driveway,' explained Loretta. 'He says it makes a mess.'

Joe saw the gravel that had been sprayed about and the deep hoof prints in the drive. Loretta's father had a point. When he looked up, Loretta was staring at him.

'Why do you stammer?' she asked.

'W-What?' said Joe. Usually people were too polite to mention his speech impediment.

'Did something traumatic happen to you when you were little?' Loretta asked curiously. From the gleam in her eye she seemed to hope it was something juicy.

'No,' said Joe. 'I've j-j-just always t-talked this way. Doctors don't know what c-c-causes it.'

'That doesn't surprise me,' said Loretta. 'There's a lot doctors don't know. My own parents in particular are startlingly ignorant of anything that takes place outside of a chest cavity.'

'It's worse when I'm n-n-n . . .' began Joe.

'Nervous,' said Loretta, finishing his sentence for him. 'And I make you nervous, don't I?'

'N-n-n . . .' Joe struggled to protest, but he couldn't get the word out.

Loretta laughed. 'Don't worry. I have that effect on everyone. I've spent years cultivating it.'

Joe fell silent. Not because he couldn't speak, but because he had no idea what to say to this very strange and beautiful girl.

'So see you later, I guess,' called Loretta as she turned to go, raising her heels ready to give Vladimir a nudge.

'Wait!' cried Joe.

Loretta turned back.

'I n-need to talk to you,' said Joe.

'Really?' said Loretta. 'How intriguing.'

'I was w-w-walking over to see you,' explained Joe.

'Then what good luck that we bumped into each other,' said Loretta happily. 'Do you want me to jump down so we can see eye-to-eye?'

'No, er . . .' Joe began to protest.

But Loretta had already swung a leg over and was sliding off Vladimir. She turned to Joe and smiled. 'What is it?' she asked.

Joe's brain had stopped working as soon as Loretta smiled.

'Er . . .' said Joe.

'It must be important for you to walk over to see me,' said Loretta.

Joe nodded.

'Do you have a problem?' asked Loretta.

Joe nodded again, happy that she was so quick on the uptake.

'What is it?' Loretta asked.

'The b-b-ball,' said Joe.

'Oh,' said Loretta. 'I understand.'

Joe sighed with relief.

'You've hit a ball into our yard and you want to go and get it,' said Loretta. 'That's fine. Pop over anytime.'

She turned to remount her horse.

'No,' said Joe. 'It's the *b-b-ball* ball.'

Loretta looked confused.

Joe took a deep breath and stared at the ground so he wouldn't be intimidated by Loretta's beauty, then said all in a hurry, 'The Cockroach Races Ball. Daisy Odinsdottir asked me to ask her, but I don't want to because she terrifies me. I told her I was taking someone else, but then she asked who and I couldn't think of any girl's name from school, so I said . . . you.'

There was a dreadful pause. Joe looked up. Loretta was staring at him again. He wished Vlad would just kick him in the head and put him out of his misery.

'You told Daisy Odinsdottir you were taking me to the Cockroach Races Ball?' clarified Loretta.

'Y-Y-Yes,' said Joe. 'I'm so sorry. I can tell her you b-b-broke your ankle and can't go. Not that that would work because then you'd have to b-b-break your ankle. But I could tell her you ch-changed your mind when you got to know me better.'

'But then she'd expect you to take her,' said Loretta.

'Yes,' said Joe. 'All the possibilities are h-h-horrible.'

'There's another possibility,' said Loretta. 'You could actually take me.'

'Oh no,' said Joe. 'I wouldn't dream of that. You're far too beautiful. It wouldn't be fair.'

'I'd like to go,' said Loretta.

'But with someone better,' said Joe.

'No,' said Loretta. 'You'll do.' She smiled at him mischievously as she remounted her horse. Her bottom flying past Joe's face with disconcerting closeness.

'Pick me up at seven,' said Loretta.

'Should I get you a c-c-corsage?' asked Joe.

'Gosh no,' said Loretta. 'This isn't the 1950s. Besides, all my dresses are too nice to stick pins in. Don't be early,' said Loretta as she kicked her horse into a trot.

'Don't you mean "Don't be late"?' asked Joe.

'No, I want to be late,' said Loretta. 'That way I can make a much more impressive entrance.'

She nudged her horse again and galloped forward, disappearing around the side of the house, no doubt to further damage Dad's flowerbeds. Loretta didn't just like making impressive entrances, she liked making impressive exits as well.

Chapter 21

THE BALL

'**D**o you think these disguises will work?' asked Fin skittishly.

It was Friday night, and he and April were walking the last couple of blocks to the town hall where the Cockroach Races Ball was being held. Fin was dressed as a unicorn and April was dressed as Rudolph the Red-Nosed Reindeer. They didn't want to know why their father had these costumes in a trunk in the attic but he did, and the costumes completely covered their bodies and faces, so they were wearing them.

'Of course they'll work,' said April aggressively. 'No one can recognise us, can they?'

'But we're pretty conspicuous,' said Fin. 'We're going to really stand out.'

'Rubbish,' said April. 'People wear all sorts of weird things to parties. No one will even notice us.'

They could hear music playing as April jogged up the front steps of the venue. Fin hurried after her, not wanting to be left behind. The Currawong Town Hall was a surprisingly grand art deco building with fake plaster copies of Grecian statues and heavy brass fittings. Fin and April crossed the lobby and pushed open the heavy double doors that led into the party.

'Oh dear,' said Fin. 'We may have made a terrible mistake.'

Everyone else at the party was dressed in black tie. The boys and men all wore tuxedos and the girls and women all wore beautiful, if somewhat old-fashioned, ball gowns.

'What is this?' asked April in disgust. 'It's like we've stepped into a crowd scene from a Fred Astaire movie.'

'Let's go home,' said Fin, panicking.

April grabbed him tightly by the wrist. 'You're not going anywhere,' she said. 'No one is going to give us a second glance. They'll all be too busy worrying about how silly they look themselves, dressed up in monkey suits and dresses that look like meringues.'

April dragged Fin further into the room. They weaved their way through the dancers, April showing uncharacteristic restraint. She only shoved two couples, demanding they get out of her way, as she progressed across the floor.

'Where are we going?' asked Fin.

'Look,' said April, pointing to the far side of the room.

Fin stood on tippy-toes. 'I can't see anything.'

'Oh, I forgot you're short,' said April. 'The cockroaches are over there.'

'At the ball?!' exclaimed Fin. 'That can't be sanitary.'

They broke through the crowd and now Fin could see for himself. A long trestle table had been set up, and down its length stretched a line of cockroaches in small aquariums, large jam jars and various sized boxes. A plaque for each contestant was neatly inscribed with the trainer's names. There must have been at least sixty cockroaches in all.

April stepped forward to get a closer look, but a burly security guard intercepted her.

'Stay behind the rope,' instructed the guard sternly.

A red velvet rope hung in front of the table, cordoning it off so that no one could get within a metre of the cockroaches.

'Security is pretty tight,' said Fin.

'If you call a velvet rope and a middle-aged man with a heart condition "security",' said April.

'Hey, I don't have a heart condition,' said the security guard.

'Really?' said April, with feigned concern. 'Then you should check with your doctor, because it's not natural to have skin that grey, and you're sweating a lot.'

'What?' asked the security guard.

'He doesn't look good, does he?' said April, nudging Fin and giving him a meaningful look.

'Have you had any shortness of breath or chest pains recently?' asked Fin, catching on and following April's lead.

'No more than usual,' said the guard.

'What about itchy feet and excessive dandruff?' asked April.

'Are they symptoms of heart disease too?'

'Oh yes,' said April sombrely. 'Towards the end.'

'If I were you, I'd drive straight to emergency right now,' said Fin.

'But I've got to look after the cockroaches,' the guard replied, starting to get distressed.

'Do you? Do you really?' said April. 'Don't you have a family? Shouldn't you be looking after yourself for their sake? Isn't that more important?'

'My wife would be angry if I had a heart attack,' worried the guard. 'She's always telling me I eat too much cheese.'

'Get to the hospital,' urged Fin. 'We'll keep an eye on the cockroaches for you.'

'You will? Thanks!' said the security guard, before hurrying away.

'Finally,' said April. 'Now we can do whatever we like with these cockroaches.'

'What is it we want to do?' asked Fin.

'Check for dead bodies for a start,' said April, opening the first box.

Suddenly, the music cut out.

April flinched and jumped back, thinking she'd been caught, but then there was the whine of feedback from a microphone and a kerfuffle up on stage. Everyone looked over to see what was happening, but April and Fin were the most horrified. It was their dad. He was wrestling the microphone out of the DJ's hands.

'Give it to me!' demanded Dad. 'I've got something I want to say!' With one good hard yank he twisted the microphone out of the DJ's grip, pulling him off-balance so he toppled over his own turntable. Dad didn't care, he turned to address the crowd. 'Can you hear me?' he asked, tapping the top of the microphone so small bangs echoed deafeningly about the room.

'Yes,' called several people from the crowd.

'I'm looking for my children,' said Dad. 'April, Fin, are you here?'

Fin started to move forward, but April grabbed him. 'Don't,' she whispered. 'We're not meant to be here, remember? We can't reveal our identities.'

'I need you,' Dad pleaded. 'Joe's been kidnapped!'

Fin broke away from April and forced his way through the crowd to the stage. Dad was still looking out, scanning the sea of faces. He wasn't expecting his children to be dressed as animals. Fin tapped him on the foot. Dad flinched when he looked down at the human-sized unicorn. 'Are you one of them?' he yelped. 'Are you with the Kolektiv?'

'No, Dad. It's me, Fin,' said Fin. He pulled open the mouth of his unicorn suit so Dad could get a glimpse of his face.

'Oh, what a relief,' said Dad. 'And what a good idea to come disguised. If only Joe had thought to do the same.' Tears started to well up in his eyes.

'What happened?' asked April. She had come over to join them.

'Can we trust the reindeer?' asked Dad.

'It's April,' said Fin. 'So probably not.'

'I was in my office repairing some chainsaw damage to the wall when I heard them coming,' said Dad.

'Heard who coming?' asked Fin.

'The Kolektiv,' said Dad. 'They came in a helicopter. My first thought was to go down to the cellar and lock myself in until they went away, but then I heard footsteps on the deck. When I looked out the window, Joe was being dragged into the helicopter and it flew off.'

'But why would anyone want to kidnap Joe?' asked April.

'To get to your mother,' said Dad. 'They can use him as leverage.'

'I don't know,' said April. 'I'm not convinced she liked him that much. I don't think it would work.'

By now the music and dancing had resumed, but there was an increasingly loud pulsating beat that didn't appear to have anything to do with the song that was playing.

'What is that?' asked Fin.

'What?' said April.

'That sound?'

'I can't hear anything,' said April. 'Maybe you're having a stroke.'

'It sounds like a helicopter,' said Fin.

'It's the Kolektiv! They've come back!' exclaimed Dad. 'Quick, run!'

He grabbed April and Fin with surprising strength for a timid horticulturist and started frogmarching them to the entrance.

'Dad, we can't leave!' protested April. 'We're investigating a crime.'

'We'll be the crime under investigation if we don't get out of here,' wailed Dad, practically pushing them down the front steps ahead of him.

But they were too late. The helicopter was deafeningly loud. It was hovering low as it came in to land. Its floodlights lit up the ground, blinding April and Fin. They couldn't run away now, because they couldn't see where they were going. They could just as easily run right into the blades of the helicopter.

'We're doomed,' groaned Dad. The fight went out of him. He still held tight to April and Fin, but now more for comfort.

Everyone else from the Cockroach Races Ball was flooding out of the hall to see what was going on.

'Buck up, Dad,' Fin yelled over the sound of the helicopter. 'They can't kidnap us with so many witnesses.'

'The only reason you say that is because you can't remember all the times your memory has been altered,' shouted Dad.

The helicopter touched down on the bitumen of the car park. The next second the door slid open and a man in a tuxedo stepped out.

'I didn't know spies really wore tuxedos like James Bond,' said April.

'That's not a spy!' exclaimed Fin. 'It's Joe!'

Joe was almost unrecognisable in a suit and neatly combed hair. He turned back to the helicopter, reached in and helped out a beautiful supermodel. Except, of course, it wasn't a real supermodel.

'That's Loretta!' exclaimed April.

'No!' cried Fin.

It was amazing Fin could speak at all. He felt like his heart was being crushed. When tectonic plates spend millennia pushing into each other with unimaginable force, the pressure is so great that the carbon in the rock is compressed into diamonds. That is how crushed Fin's heart felt in his chest at that exact moment, like it was being crushed so hard it could form a diamond.

Loretta and Joe swept towards them. Joe holding her tightly as if worried that this terrifyingly beautiful girl would be blown away by the down thrust of the helicopter.

The crowd parted, except for Fin. April had to yank him out of the way. Then the crowd flowed back into the hall like the tide returning. Everyone chattering excitedly with a new buzz of exhilaration in the air.

'What just happened?' asked Dad, beginning to wonder if his oldest and least-articulate child really was a spy. The tuxedo did seem to be a uniform for those people. It wouldn't be the first time a spy had snuck past him and infiltrated his family. That was what his wife had done. Dad turned and looked at the helicopter. 'Is that my helicopter? And was that the girl from next door flying it?'

Dad reached in, turned the engine off and took out the keys.

'Loretta had to make a dramatic entrance,' sniped April. 'She does everything dramatically.' This really was the pot calling the kettle black, because April had quite the flair for dramatics herself.

'Ah, Mr Peski, I presume,' said Mr Lang, walking down the front steps of the town hall towards Dad. 'We meet at last.'

'Are you Kolektiv?' asked Dad in alarm.

'Close,' said April. 'He's the school guidance counsellor.'

'Is that your helicopter?' asked Mr Lang, nodding at the keys in Dad's hand.

'I'm not breaking any government regulations,' said Dad defensively.

'Okay,' said Mr Lang, 'but the reason I ask is because at this year's Cockroach Races there's going to be a display of "Aviation through the Ages".'

'What's that got to do with cockroaches?' sneered April.

'Cockroaches have wings,' said Mr Lang. 'They fly. Come with me, Mr Peski. I want to discuss the logistics of putting your helicopter on display.'

Mr Lang took Dad by the arm in the experienced manner of a teacher used to grabbing hold of a child so they can't get away. He led Dad back inside the hall.

'I want to go home,' said Fin hoarsely.

'What about our investigation?!' exclaimed April. 'We've barely begun.'

'I don't care anymore,' said Fin. He turned away and started trudging towards their house. He would have looked like a dramatic figure himself if he hadn't been dressed as a unicorn.

Chapter 22

DEPRESSED

Fin was sitting at the kitchen counter, trying to encourage their cockroach to run towards the piece of cheese he had put out for her. He wished his mum was there. April was fine if you needed someone to seek violent retribution, but Mum always cooked such emotionally supportive pancakes.

'I'm so depressed,' he said.

'I know,' agreed April. 'She's a terrible cockroach. She never runs anywhere.'

'*Woof!*' barked Pumpkin as he lunged forward to bite the cockroach. He disliked it when April showed affection for anything other than him. Fortunately, she rarely did.

'No, I'm depressed about tonight,' said Fin.

'Totally,' agreed April. 'We were so close to inspecting those cockroaches. If only Joe and Loretta hadn't turned up.'

'Yeah,' agreed Fin. 'It's all Joe's stupid fault.'

'I'd blame Loretta more,' said April. 'She's the one who knew how to fly the helicopter.'

'He knew how I felt about her and he stole her from me,' muttered Fin.

'What?' asked April, not following Fin's half of the conversation. 'He didn't know you hated every particle of her nauseatingly perfect body?'

Fin looked at April. It suddenly occurred to him that his infuriatingly self-involved younger sister may not have noticed his infatuation with their impossibly attractive next-door neighbour. 'You know what, April. For once I'm glad you are a totally self-absorbed monomaniac.'

'Don't get all mushy on me,' said April, punching Fin on the arm.

221

Fin smiled. His arm would bruise, but he knew a punch that light was as close as his sister came to a gesture of affection.

'So what are we going to do about these mysterious cockroach deaths?' he asked. 'The town still blames us for the killing spree.'

'We're never going to be able to figure it out using reason and logic,' said April.

'Because we're not smart enough?' said Fin.

'No, dummy. Because no one in this town is reasonable or logical.'

'But we've got to clear our names,' said Fin. 'I know you don't like the kids here, I don't particularly like them either, but I can't go through the next five years of school being hated by everyone.'

They heard the front door open and Dad bustled in.

'You!' said April, pointing at him.

'What have I done?' panicked Dad.

'You've got a lot of junk about the place,' said April. 'Do you think you could build us a couple of bicycles?'

'I suppose so,' said Dad uncertainly.

'Come on,' said April. 'If you can whip up a helicopter, something with two wheels and a chain can't be too hard.'

'Well, yes, in fact, I've got some old bike frames in my shed,' remembered Dad.

'Excellent,' said April. 'This will work perfectly.'

'What are you on about?' asked Fin.

'I've got a plan,' she announced.

'You do?' said Fin, surprised. His sister was more of a 'punch now, ask questions later' kind of girl. Definitely not a 'think hard and come up with a structured response' type.

'We're going to set a trap,' said April, her eyes sparkling with menace.

Fin was suspicious. 'You're not thinking about one of those bear traps, are you? With the razor-sharp steel jaws that slam shut. Because I'm pretty sure those are illegal.'

'No, not one of those,' said April impatiently. 'The shipping was too expensive.'

'What?!' exclaimed Fin. 'You tried to get one?'

'Yeah,' said April. 'Last year when I was sure you were sneaking into my room to copy my maths homework.'

'But that wasn't me,' said Fin. 'It was Joe sneaking into your room to use your pencil sharpener.'

April shrugged. 'It would have worked either way. If I'd broken your leg, Joe would have felt bad and confessed. But that's not the type of trap I'm planning to use.'

Just then the house started to vibrate. In the distance they could hear the loud *thwack-thwack-thwack* of an approaching helicopter.

'Joe's coming home,' said April.

'Harrumph,' said Fin.

The noise became deafeningly loud. Through the kitchen window they could see tree branches getting whipped about and even torn off by the down thrust.

The helicopter lowered into view, carefully touching down right in the middle of Dad's best rose bed. If the wind hadn't flattened every living plant, then the runners of the chopper grinding them into the soil certainly did. The engine cut out and the blades began to slow.

The door slid open and Joe jumped out. Loretta got out too. She reached up and kissed Joe on the cheek. In the kitchen Fin stood up, his fists clenched as he watched them. Joe held his hand over his cheek and watched Loretta walk away.

Joe turned and made his way to the back door.

'Why did she land the helicopter in the middle of the flowerbed?' demanded April, as soon as Joe stepped in through the back door.

'She said it was important to have a t-t-target to aim for,' said Joe.

'How could you?' demanded Fin. His arms were crossed and he glared at his big brother.

'What?' asked Joe. 'I'll help D-Dad replant.'

'Ignore him,' said April. 'He's just annoyed because I wanted to break his leg. I've got a plan for tomorrow and I need your help. The first thing we have to do is make two cockroach costumes.'

Chapter 23

THE COCKROACH RACES

The morning dawned of the Currawong Cockroach Races. The weather was perfect: bright blue skies, warm but not too warm. Optimal cockroach scurrying temperatures. That is, optimal temperatures for normal-sized cockroaches, not for two kids dressed as cockroaches and riding home-made bikes into town.

Although, arguably, no temperature is ideal for someone dressed in a cockroach costume riding a bicycle. Mimicking a cockroach's exoskeleton with household items had been no easy task. Cockroaches have surprisingly complicated bodies. Fin and April had used tin cans for the leg joints and fishing line to string the extra legs to their arms so they would move in unison. Then they'd made wings out of sheets of cardboard, spray-painted brown, and finished the whole thing off with brown bicycle helmets, ski goggles for eyes and coat-hangers for antennae. They may not have looked exactly like cockroaches to a trained entomologist, but they didn't look like April and Fin, which was really the main point of the exercise.

Dad had done a pretty good job on their bicycles. They didn't look store-bought but they worked.

'Hurry up,' urged April. 'We can't be late.'

'My legs aren't as long as yours,' grumbled Fin. 'This isn't easy.' A tin can was starting to cut into the back of his calf.

'It's not my fault you're a leprechaun,' said April. 'Just pedal harder.' She accelerated away, leaving Fin desperately trying to keep up.

The Viswanathan's electric car sped past them, honking its horn.

'There go Joe and Loretta,' said Fin glumly.

Joe and Pumpkin were travelling to the races separately. They couldn't be seen with April and Fin in case someone guessed who the giant cockroaches were and kicked them out.

'You shouldn't complain,' said April. 'Imagine poor Joe, stuck in the car with Loretta and her crazy Swedish au pair having to make small talk.'

'Yeah,' said Fin sarcastically. 'Poor Joe, stuck with Loretta and a tall blonde, beautiful Swedish woman.'

'Maybe Pumpkin will bite them,' said April hopefully.

When they got to the gardens, April and Fin were astonished to see the size of the crowds. There was a line of people hundreds of metres long winding around the block. The queue slowly shuffled forward towards the entrance.

'Why don't they just climb over the fence?' wondered April.

The gardens were contained by a three-foot picket fence. It couldn't stop a determined turtle. Any adult or large child could step over it if they wanted to.

'The people here are too honest.' Fin sighed.

'Suckers,' said April contemptuously. She stepped forward and swung her can-encased leg over the nearest part of the fence.

'Don't do that!' exclaimed Fin, grabbing hold of her arm.

'Let go of me,' said April, shoving Fin. 'People will notice if you make a fuss, you big twerp.'

'No, I mean you don't need to,' said Fin. 'Look, competitors have their own entrance with no queue.'

April glanced over. There was a small gate with 'COMPETITORS' ENTRANCE' written over it.

'So we're banned, but our cockroach has a special entrance?' she asked.

'Our cockroach isn't suspected of mass insecticide,' reasoned Fin.

'This town treats cockroaches better than people,' April muttered, as she swung her leg back and straightened her cockroach costume with as much dignity as she could muster. Then she picked up their cockroach and headed towards the gate.

▬▬▬

As they entered the gardens there was a palpable feeling of excitement in the air. Competitors protectively hovered over their cockroaches. Spectators milled about, buying snacks, checking out the aviation display and jostling for the best spots in one of the four big sets of raised seating.

'Wow,' said Fin. 'I was expecting something small scale, but this is more like a gladiator's battle pit.'

'I could understand if there were people being eaten by lions,' said April, shaking her head. 'But it's just going to be tiny cockroaches. Most of the crowd will barely be able to see what's going on.'

'Yes, they will,' said Fin. 'Look, there's a jumbotron.'

Between two banks of seating was a huge display. Each racer in turn was flashing up on the screen alongside a list of their statistics as they were read out by the announcer.

'*Boadicea. Owners – Lily Dalecki. Age – two months. Length – 32 mm. Top speed – 52 cm/sec.*'

'Look, there's Madge!' exclaimed April in delight, as the details of their own cockroach flashed up.

'You named our cockroach "Madge"?' asked Fin.

'She looks like a Madge,' said April.

'*Madge. Owners – Fin and April Peski,*' said the announcer. '*Age – unknown. Length – unknown. Top speed – unknown.*'

'That's a bit harsh,' said April. 'It makes it sound like we don't know our cockroach very well.

'We don't,' said Fin.

'We know she was extremely hard to extract from our next-door neighbour's microwave,' said April. 'They need to have a category for that.'

Fin wandered over to the raised racing platform in the centre of the banks of seating.

'That must be the famous ceremonial shield,' he said, pointing to what looked like a large wok lid.

'Let me have a look at that,' said April. She picked it up by the rim and carefully rubbed the handle. She turned her back to the crowd so she could get a closer look without anyone watching. 'Not exactly high-tech is it?'

'Better put that down,' said a laconic voice. It was Coach Voss.

'What are you doing here?' asked April rudely, turning back around.

'Shhh,' hissed Fin. 'We're in disguise, remember.'

April replaced the shield and they walked away.

April and Fin had a look around the rest of the gardens. There were a variety of stalls selling all sorts of local produce: doughnuts, fresh lemonade and wildly overpriced chutney. But the highlight was in the far corner of the gardens. The aviation display. Someone had set up a hot air balloon. It looked magnificent – a rainbow of silk swaying in the breeze. For a dollar kids could have a ride, which involved sitting in the basket while the balloon was raised three metres off the ground and then lowered back down again.

Set up next to the hot air balloon was an old propeller plane, a glider and finally Dad's helicopter. Dad was sitting alongside it, but so no one could approach him, particularly not with a cockroach, he was inside what looked like an old-fashioned telephone box, except it was made entirely of clear perspex. A placard on the box read:

This helicopter has been loaned to the aviation display thanks to Harold Peski. As a courtesy, please do not allow any cockroaches inside the helicopter.

'Hi, Dad,' called Fin.

Dad did not look up from the book he was reading.

'That's rude,' said April.

April banged on the perspex box to get his attention. Dad looked up and saw two giant cockroaches standing in front of him. He screamed in terror. At least they assumed he did. They couldn't hear it, they could only see it.

He doesn't recognise us in our disguises,' said Fin. 'He thinks we're giant cockroaches.'

April rolled her eyes. 'For a parent, Dad is really hard work.' She lifted her ski goggles to show her face. Dad clutched his chest in relief, then he tapped the telephone receiver hanging next to him. Fin noticed there was another receiver on the outside. He picked it up. Dad did the same.

'Hi, Dad,' Fin said into the receiver.

'Promise me you'll be careful,' said Dad. 'This place is infested with cockroaches.'

'We will,' said Fin. 'Are you okay in there? Have you got enough oxygen?'

'Yes, yes,' said Dad. He pointed to a gas canister on the floor. 'I have my own bottled supply in case the Kolektiv attack us with gas.'

'That would be pretty unlikely though, wouldn't it, Dad?' said April.

'That's when they strike,' said Dad. 'When you least expect it.'

'*Could all competitors for heat one kindly make their way to the arena,*' came a request over the PA system.

'That's us,' said Fin.

'Time to catch a cockroach killer,' said April malevolently.

Chapter 24

EVERYTHING GOES WRONG

There were six heats with ten cockroaches in each race. The winner of each race would go through to the final. Mr Lang was the commentator. He introduced each cockroach as it was placed under the ceremonial shield. A Japanese translator was standing off to the side, giving live translations for viewers at home.

Coach Voss was the master of ceremonies. It was his job to make sure all the cockroaches went under the ceremonial shield and then call out, 'On your marks, get set, GO!' as he whipped off the covering. The cockroaches didn't understand English, but it added to the drama of the occasion and made sure everyone in the crowd was paying attention.

From the first heat on things did not go to plan. In heat one, as soon as the shield was whipped off, it was clear something was wrong with one of the cockroaches. As the other nine sprinted for the line, the cockroach limped around in circles.

'Dobby's Boy is struggling,' said Mr Lang. 'Looks like he may have pulled a hamstring.'

'Do cockroaches even have hamstrings?' asked April.

Animesh rushed forward and gently lifted his roach out of the arena. 'What's wrong, boy?' he asked as he looked him over. Kieran was looking closely too. 'Look! He's only got five legs. Someone has ripped his leg off!'

There were gasps from the crowd.

'It must have been an accident,' said Mr Lang, 'or perhaps one of the other roaches did it. Coach Voss, you're the master of ceremonies. What do you think?'

Coach Voss thought for a moment. 'Terrible tragedy, but Nelly's Grin is the winner,' he said, with his usual brevity.

The crowd muttered among themselves.

In heat two the trouble continued. The favourite was King Richard, and when the ceremonial shield was lifted he didn't moved a millimetre. Close inspection revealed the cockroach had been stuck down with superglue.

In heat three the hotly tipped Ali's Barber was found chomping on a piece of pepperoni while the other roaches ran off.

In heat four the short-odds contender, Marky Markus, disappeared completely.

Then, in the final heat, when Coach Voss whipped off the lid the cockroaches showed no interest in running for the line whatsoever. They were too busy writhing all over each other.

'Are they wrestling?' asked April.

'I don't think so,' said Fin.

'The cockroaches appear to be covered in some substance,' said Mr Lang. He leaned in and sniffed. 'It's honey.'

One cockroach seemed to be less affected than the rest. It staggered away from the group and started making its way towards the line.

'Which one is that?' asked Mr Lang, consulting his notes. 'Madge! Madge is in the lead.'

'That's our cockroach!' exclaimed April.

'Shhh,' said Fin. 'Keep your voice down or some-one will recognise us.'

'Madge isn't moving fast, but there's not much competition,' said Mr Lang. The other roaches were still trying to eat the honey off each other.

'Good ole Madge,' cried April. 'She's going to win!'

'And she does it!' exclaimed Mr Lang. 'Madge wins the last heat. And that roach is owned by . . .' Mr Lang checked his notes. 'Fin and April Peski?!'

There were boos from the crowd.

'They rigged it!' cried Matilda, leaping to her feet.

'They can't have done,' said Mr Lang. 'They're not even here.'

'Stop!' cried April. 'I know who did it!'

Everyone fell silent and looked at April.

'Who are you?' asked Constable Pike. He was standing by the racing dais overseeing security.

April realised she was still wearing the cockroach suit. She pulled off her ski goggles and brown bicycle helmet.

'I am April Peski,' declared April. 'And I know who has been secretly killing cockroaches.'

Everyone gasped. There was muttering among the crowd as people discussed who April was and why she was disguised as a giant insect.

'Of course you do!' accused Matilda. 'Because it's you.'

'You're banned from these gardens,' said Constable Pike. 'I'm arresting you for breaking council regulations pertaining to special festivals.'

'You can't arrest someone for that,' said Fin. 'It's not a proper law. All you can do is fine her. Oh, and me, because I'm Fin Peski.' Fin removed his ski goggles and bicycle helmet too.

There were more gasps.

'Right, I'm telling your dad about this!' declared Constable Pike.

'Good luck,' said April. 'He's afraid of authority figures. He'll run away when he sees your uniform.'

'April, just t-t-tell us who did it,' called Joe. He was sitting with Loretta in the middle of a stand. 'Before you get yourself in more trouble.'

Pumpkin barked excitedly and leapt down from Loretta's lap to hurry over to his mistress. When April started yelling at people it usually meant he would soon get to start biting ankles.

'The culprit is . . .' April paused for dramatic effect, which was totally unnecessary because everyone in the thousands-strong crowd was already hanging on her every word. 'Constable Pike!'

There was a collective intake of breath.

'But that doesn't make sense,' said Mr Lang. 'No one has been more devastated than Constable Pike by the recent spate of cockroach deaths.'

'Exactly!' said April. 'He's been overcompensating.'

'Do you have any evidence?' asked Mr Lang.

'It fits perfectly,' declared April. 'How else do you explain his totally incompetent investigation and unprofessional accusations of innocent children?'

'Perhaps he's just incompetent and unprofessional,' suggested Fin.

'No way. He's obviously got deep-seated psychological issues about cockroach races. He's a serial cockroach-killing psychopath. Probably the only reason he became a cop was so he'd be in a position to carry out these devious crimes. Someone citizen's arrest him before he escapes,' cried April. She turned and looked at Joe.

'Don't look at me,' said Joe. 'I'm not going anywhere near him. He's a cop. He carries a gun.'

'You can't accuse the one member of the police force in this town,' said Mr Lang.

'I can too,' said April, 'because I have proof.'

'This is ridiculous,' said Constable Pike. 'It's an insult. After all I've done for the Cockroach Races.'

'I knew someone other than me was killing the cockroaches,' said April. 'So I laid a trap to catch them.'

'She didn't get a bear trap, did she?' called Joe from his seat.

'No, the shipping was too expensive,' Fin assured him.

'When I inspected the ceremonial shield earlier,' continued April, 'I put purple food colouring paste on the underside of the handle. Anyone who touches it will get the paste on their skin and their fingers will turn purple. I can prove that Constable Pike is the culprit because when he turns his hands over we will all see that he has purple fingers.'

Everyone looked at Constable Pike. 'You can't take her seriously,' he protested.

'Just show us your hands, Bob,' said Mr Lang.

Constable Pike turned over his hands and the skin was . . . a completely normal shade of pink.

'No way!' exclaimed April. 'I could have sworn it was you.'

Someone in the crowd booed. Soon there was a whole chorus of boos.

'We are never going to live this down,' muttered Fin. 'We're all going to have to live in another town.'

'It's okay,' said April, still irrationally confident. 'Then it must be the only other obvious suspect!'

'Who?' asked Constable Pike.

'Don't encourage her,' pleaded Fin.

'The cockroach killer must be . . .' April swivelled about, looking for the right person in the crowd. 'Daisy Odinsdottir!'

Everyone gasped. Daisy's face appeared on the jumbotron. She looked horrified and confused.

'But she hasn't got a motive,' said Fin.

'She did it because she's deranged and evil,' said April. 'There's no other explanation why she would have chased our brother, Joe, around school all week, goggling at him with stupid moony eyes.'

Daisy was looking very embarrassed now. So was Joe. Loretta was loving it.

'Daisy actually cornered Joe in the boys' toilets!' revealed April. 'You'd have to be deranged and have no sense of smell to go in there.'

People started muttering. 'Show us your hands,' called a voice from the crowd.

Daisy slowly held up her hands and turned them palm out to the camera. They were a normal pink colour.

'What?!' exclaimed April. 'That can't be right.'

'That's enough,' said Constable Pike.

'No, someone here has purple fingers!' said April. She whirled round to confront the entire crowd. 'Everyone show me your hands.'

'Great. Now you're accusing the whole town,' said Fin.

But everyone in the raised seats was curious to see if their hands had changed colour. They were looking for themselves and showing their neighbours. Everyone's hands were still pink or brown, depending on what colour their skin was in the first place.

'No one?' asked April. 'Someone here must have purple hands. Someone tampered with those cockroaches and to do so they had to lift the lid.'

'Then your trap proves that no one here did that,' said Mr Lang.

'I reckon it's all just a story,' said Animesh, 'to hide the fact that she did it.'

People in the crowd began to yell 'Yeah!', 'Arrest her!' and 'Cockroach killer!'.

'Wait!' cried Joe, standing up in his seat. The need to protect his sister imbued him with clarity and confidence. 'My sister may be deranged, unstable and deeply unpleasant. She may have violent tendencies, a menacing presence and an abusive manner . . .'

April nodded. It was all true.

'But she isn't a liar,' said Joe. 'Someone here must have purple hands.'

Fin gasped. 'I know who did it!'

Now everyone was looking at him.

'Coach Voss!' said Fin.

Everyone turned to look at Coach Voss's hands. He turned them over. The fingers on his right hand were bright purple.

There were gasps in the crowd.

'Of course he touched the ceremonial shield,' said Constable Pike. 'He's the master of ceremonies. It's his job to start each race by lifting the lid.'

'Which also gives him unparalleled access to the racers,' accused Fin. 'He had more opportunity than anyone else.'

'Enough!' snapped Mr Lang. 'You can't accuse Coach Voss. He is the greatest lawn bowler this town has seen since the legendary Sir Roland himself.'

'But he's also Matilda's great-uncle, aren't you?' asked Fin, turning to Coach Voss.

'What?' asked April.

'Matilda's full name is Matilda Voss-Nevers,' said Fin. 'They're related.'

'Wow, this town has a pretty shallow gene pool,' said April.

'And Matilda said she had a great-uncle who had never lived down the shame of losing the cockroach races many years ago,' said Fin. 'Was that you, Coach Voss?'

Coach Voss stared in stunned silence.

'But that's not a motive,' said Constable Pike.

'It is if you hold a grudge for seventy years,' said Fin. 'The Currawong Cockroach Races are big business now. People follow them all around the world. So when a bookmaker asks you to rig the races, finally you have a chance to make a whole load of money and get revenge.'

'You're making it up,' said Coach Voss. 'You've got no proof. You're the kids no one likes. I'm a respected pillar of this community.'

'Then you won't mind if we check your phone messages, will you?' said April, waggling his phone in her hand.

Coach Voss clutched his pocket. 'Hey! How did you get that?'

'If you're going to leave it lying around in your pocket,' said April, 'you're practically begging for me to steal it.'

'Hey! Give that back!' bellowed Coach Voss.

'Make me,' mocked April as she danced away, scrolling through the apps. 'Here we go, most recent messages.' She suddenly stopped moving. 'Oh my gosh. Fin's actually right! It says . . . "Captain McGoo in the second". And the message before that is "Dinkston's Pride in the first". Each message came through exactly two minutes before each race.'

'Let me see that,' said Constable Pike. 'The texts are from an international number. They start with 81. What country is that?'

'Japan!' cried Loretta. 'I've got cousins living there.'

'Cockroach racing is huge in Japan,' said April. 'Someone over there is arranging to have the races fixed.'

Constable Pike turned to Coach Voss. He looked heartbroken. 'Coach, why would you do it?'

'For the money, you idiot,' snarled Coach Voss. A menacing glare came over his face. 'Do you think I like having to coach snotty teenagers for an hourly rate? After all I've given to the sport of lawn bowls,

I'm just a tourist attraction. I'm no different to the giant poo, except the poo doesn't have bills to pay.'

'Coach, I'm sorry. I'm going to have to put you under arrest,' said Constable Pike, his voice cracking as he spoke. He looked like he was about to start crying.

'Ha! You'll have to catch me first,' said Coach Voss. Then, with surprising agility for a man of his age, he spun on his heel and made a run for it.

The constable was fumbling to blow his nose and didn't react straightaway, and since everyone else was expecting him to handle the situation there was a moment of hesitation.

'Quick, someone stop him!' yelled April.

Unfortunately, the average person is inherently reluctant to crash-tackle an octogenarian, no matter how wicked he might be. Joe got to his feet, responding to his sister's cry, but he was in the middle of the crowd so he had to politely say 'excuse me' ten times and wait for everyone in his row to tuck their knees in before he could get out.

April and Fin took off after Coach Voss with Constable Pike close behind, but the coach had already made it to the hot air balloon in the corner of the gardens. He vaulted into the basket and yanked free the tethers, one after another.

'Stop!' cried Fin.

April was closest. She leapt forward to grab hold of the basket but her fingertips just skimmed the outside of the wicker as the balloon lifted up off the ground. Pumpkin ran right over the top of her, yapping and bravely leaping at the basket himself. But he was only thirty centimetres tall, so he didn't get far off the ground before crashing down onto April's head.

By the time Constable Pike and Fin had caught up, and April was back on her feet, the balloon was already several metres up in the air. Joe ran over and leapt as high as he could, but he only managed to nudge the basket with his hands. There was nothing for him to grab on to.

'When I was a boy the Cockroach Cup was stolen from me,' yelled Coach Voss, his voice full of emotion. 'I never forgive and I never forget!'

With that, he reached up and tugged on the fuel line. A burst of flame billowed up and the hot air balloon accelerated fractionally. It was slowly and gracefully raising into the sky. The rest of the crowd had made their way over now. Several thousand people were gathered, watching the balloon gradually drift away.

'This has to be the slowest criminal getaway ever in history,' said Fin.

April turned to the crowd. 'Is there anybody here who has a grappling hook?

No one responded.

'When have you ever seen a grappling hook anywhere other than in a cartoon?' asked Fin.

'Well, it would be totally useful if we had one right now!' said April. 'We've got a deranged lunatic making the slowest escape imaginable. If we had a big heavy hook, we could just pull him back down here.'

A sandbag thudded to the ground, narrowly missing April's head. 'Hey!' she cried, looking up.

'I can hear you,' said Coach Voss. 'I heard you call me a deranged lunatic.'

'Well, you are one,' said April.

Another sandbag hurtled downwards, straight at April. Luckily, Joe had fast reflexes and by pushing his sister hard to the ground the sandbag just missed her.

'That hurt!' April yelled at Joe.

'A sandbag on the head would have hurt more.' Joe shrugged.

'We've got to stop him,' said Fin. 'He's moving slowly now, but once he gets higher up the winds are faster. He'll be crossing the coast in a couple of hours.'

'There's nothing we can do,' said April. 'We don't have a grappling hook, and Constable Pike is too much of a wimp to shoot him down.'

'It's my job to uphold the law, not break it,' protested Constable Pike.

'Like I said,' said April. 'A wimp.'

'If only we had another hot air balloon,' said Fin. 'We could give chase.'

'We do have a h-h-helicopter,' Joe pointed out, 'and Loretta knows how to fly it.'

'That sounds like fun!' said Loretta, joining them. 'I'm so glad your family moved to Currawong. You have the best ideas for group activities.'

'Let's go!' said April.

April, Fin, Joe, Pumpkin and Loretta ran over to Dad's helicopter.

'I can't condone this!' yelled Constable Pike.

'Quick, Loretta,' said April. 'Turn the helicopter on so we can't hear Constable Boring-Pants.'

Loretta put on the headset and flicked a few switches. The engine rumbled to life and the rotors slowly began to turn, rapidly accelerating to a whip-like pace. The crowd fell back to give the helicopter, and its alarmingly young pilot, plenty of room.

'Let's rock and roll!' cried Loretta, with a crazed gleam in her eye.

Chapter 25

THE CHASE

As Loretta pushed in the throttle and pulled back the joystick, the helicopter lifted off the ground. They flew up high above the gardens. Soon they could see the whole town from a bird's-eye view.

'Currawong really is tiny,' said Fin, looking out the window.

'Over there,' said Joe, pointing to the east. The hot air balloon was just above them and travelling quickly now on the higher winds. It was already several kilometres away. But several kilometres isn't far for a helicopter.

'Roger that,' said Loretta. She adjusted the controls and they took off after the deranged lawn bowls coach.

Up ahead, the balloon was rising swiftly. Coach Voss had the fuel on full throttle and the thinner the air, the quicker it rose.

'What are we going to do when we catch up with him?' asked Fin.

'Do you want me to ram him with the helicopter?' asked Loretta.

'No!' cried Joe.

'We'd probably get in trouble if we murdered him,' reasoned April.

'Plus we'd die when the helicopter got tangled in the balloon and plummeted to the ground,' said Fin.

'So what's the p-p-plan?' asked Joe.

'Get above him,' said April. 'I've got an idea.'

Loretta yanked the joystick back and the helicopter started flying upwards at a forty-five-degree angle. The others were pushed back into their seats by the acceleration.

'We're going to crash!' exclaimed Fin.

'Silly-billy,' said Loretta. 'I never crash.'

'You crash through Dad's flowerbeds all the time with your horse,' said Fin.

'That's the horse, not me,' said Loretta.

The helicopter straightened out and was travelling directly upwards now. It rose past the basket of the balloon.

The coach shook his fist and yelled something abusive at them, but they couldn't hear over the noise of the rotors. Although if you could read lips it was something like, 'You pesky Peski kids!'

The helicopter kept rising alongside the plump rainbow-striped silk of the balloon. As they passed the widest point the blades came dangerously close, but did not quite touch the fabric. Then they were in the clear blue sky above it.

'Now move over the top,' urged April, as she tied Pumpkin to a seat.

Loretta adjusted the controls. Now the helicopter was moving upwards at the same speed as the balloon, but positioned directly above it. The downforce of the helicopter was making the top of the balloon buffet and ripple.

'Perfect,' said April, unbuckling her own seatbelt.

'What are you d-d-doing?' panicked Joe.

'Going to get him, duh,' said April, as she slid open the door.

'You're out of your mind!' yelled Fin.

'Yes, I am,' agreed April, before leaping out.

'Nooooo!' cried Joe, frantically trying to get his own seatbelt undone.

Fin slipped out of his first, clambered to the door and looked down. April was lying flat on her back on top of the huge balloon with a big grin on her face. She bounced up and down a bit. The top of the balloon was like a huge jumping castle.

Suddenly, the helicopter was hit by a gust of wind. Loretta jerked the controls to compensate. She couldn't afford to get any closer to the balloon, but Fin's hands were so sweaty from fear that they slipped on the doorjamb. He fell. He scrunched his eyes shut tight. If he was going to die, he didn't want to see, but then it was like he hit a giant pillow. He opened his eyes and there was his crazy sister smiling at him.

'Fun, hey?!' she bellowed.

The balloon was covered in a large rope net. This gave it stability, but also acted like a climbing rig. April grabbed hold of the ropes and started climbing down the rungs. Fin did not want to be left alone on top of a hot air balloon thousands of feet in the air, so he followed.

Up in the helicopter, Joe didn't know what to do. He had no idea what April was thinking. He didn't see how jumping onto a hot air balloon could possibly help matters at all. He also didn't understand why people were so upset about someone killing cock-roaches. But deep inside his chest a primal brotherly instinct stirred. If something dreadful was going to happen to his brother and sister (as it surely was), he couldn't let it happen to them alone. He glanced back at Loretta. She turned and caught his eye. She really was stunningly beautiful. That was Joe's last thought before he threw himself out of the door.

Joe was not quite as good a shot as April and Fin. He missed the top of the balloon and skidded straight over the side. Survival instincts kicked in and Joe desperately scrabbled at the side of the balloon. His grip locked on to one of the ropes and he was able to catch himself before he fell.

Joe hung on to the side, gripping so tight he could see the balloon tremble in front of his face because of the uncontrollable shaking of his hands.

'Nice one, Joe,' said April enthusiastically.

It was quieter now. The helicopter had pulled away. April's voice sounded normal, like they were in their kitchen at home. Joe hoped he wasn't dead and that the angels in heaven didn't sound like April. That would be too cruel. He cautiously turned his head and saw his sister beaming at him. She was holding on to the ropes casually as if she were playing on the monkey bars in a playground, not hanging impossibly high in the sky.

'Come on,' said April. 'Let's get him.'

At that moment, Joe wished with all his heart that his sister had been swapped at birth with a quieter baby. He wanted to be supportive but his fingers wouldn't unclench, so there was no way he was going anywhere.

Suddenly, something stamped down on Joe's head. 'Ow!' He looked up to see Fin standing on him.

'Get out of the way, Joe,' said Fin. 'We can't hang here all day.'

Joe realised he was now holding the rope one handed because he'd released his other hand to rub his head. Now that his hand was moving, he was able to persuade the rest of his body to follow suit as he slowly and nervously descended towards the basket.

April was already at the bottom edge of the balloon waiting for him and Fin.

'Let's all swing into the basket together,' she whispered.

Joe was horrified. He didn't want to swing anywhere. He could drop or stagger or carefully lower, but he didn't want to 'swing'. He caught a glimpse of the ground far below them. They must be hundreds of metres up now. The trees and buildings looked like tiny toys.

'On the count of three,' said April. 'One . . . two . . .'

At that moment, there was another gust of wind and the balloon lurched to one side. Fin lost his grip and dropped.

'Aaagghh!' he cried.

'No!' bellowed Joe. He snatched Fin's wrist as he fell past. Fin clutched on to his brother's forearm with both hands.

Coach Voss leaned out of the balloon and saw them all hanging there.

'What are you doing?' he demanded.

'Yoga,' said April sarcastically. 'What do you think we're doing, you nitwit. We're trying to stop you!'

'No way, I'm not going to prison,' said Coach Voss. He ducked back into the basket and returned a moment later with a long pole that had a hook on the end. 'Get out of here.'

He started poking Joe and Fin with the hook.

'Hey!' cried Joe. 'You're going to kill us!'

'Not my problem,' said Coach Voss, giving Joe a hard poke in the foot.

'I'm losing my grip!' wailed Fin. His sweaty hands were slipping down Joe's arm.

'Throw him in the basket,' urged April.

'I'm not as strong as you think I am,' said Joe.

'You're supposed to take on superhuman powers when a family member's life is at stake,' said April.

'Well, obviously I don't love you two enough because right now I haven't got X-ray vision or the ability to leap tall buildings with a single bound,' said Joe.

'Fine!' said April. 'I'll handle it.'

April released her grip and slid down the last couple of metres of the balloon before grabbing the edge, swinging out from the basket then back in.

'You're out of your mind!' cried Coach Voss.

'Yes, I am,' said April as she kicked the coach with both feet squarely in the chest, then let go and dropped into the basket.

Fin completely lost his grip, slipped out of Joe's hand and landed hard on his bottom on top of the coach's head. Joe followed, awkwardly clambering down and treading on Fin and the coach as he scrambled in after them.

'You're under c-c-citizen's arrest,' said Joe, standing over the coach.

'Eeerrrgh,' moaned Coach Voss, displaying all the symptoms of concussion.

'Well done,' said April. 'Good work, everyone.'

'Um, quick question,' said Fin, glancing over the side of the basket. 'Since we just gave a serious head injury to the only person who knows how to fly this thing, do either of you know how to land a hot air balloon?'

There was a pause.

'Mum would know,' said Joe. 'I bet it's something they learn at spy school.'

'It can't be too hard,' said April. 'It's three-hundred-year-old technology.'

'Have you got C-C-Coach Voss's phone still?' asked Joe. 'We could look it up on the internet.'

'Yeah right,' said Fin. 'Currawong doesn't get mobile reception on the ground. It's not going to work up here.'

'If we turn this flame thing off, the balloon will cool and we'll go down,' said April, grabbing hold of the switch. 'It's simple thermodynamics plus gravity. Easy-peasy.' She pulled the control hard and the balloon immediately began to drop.

'Oh no!' said Fin.

'Turn it back on!' cried Joe.

April fiddled with the switch. 'It won't relight. Does anyone have a match?'

Luckily for the Peski kids, a slowly deflating hot air balloon does not drop very quickly, and they were luckier still because a strong southerly gust of wind blew them right over Wakagala Dam. So the only real danger they were in was from drowning, because after their crashlanding they were too busy fighting with each other to swim for shore. By the time a local fisherman brought his motorboat over to help, April and Fin were too exhausted to swim anywhere and Joe was hanging on to them, one under each arm, desperately trying to keep afloat.

Coach Voss had regained consciousness immediately on tumbling into the water and made a second escape bid by swimming to the bank, running up the road and attempting to hitchhike. But it was not to be. The rural Currawong area was not heavily populated at the best of times, and there was zero population on the country road that day because everyone had gone into town to watch the cockroach races. As a result the first car along the road was Constable Pike searching for the hot air balloon, and he was more than happy to pick up Coach Voss and handcuff him into the back seat.

Chapter 26

THE KEY

Yet again, there was a huge crowd at Currawong Gardens. Joe, Fin, April and Loretta were wearing their very best outfits, and since the smartest thing they owned was their school uniforms that is what they had on. Even Pumpkin had a bow on his collar to make him look extra-specially adorable. They were standing in the rotunda next to the mayor, Rowena Albright, as she gave a speech that blathered on and on. Everyone in town was there. Thousands of people filled the stands that were still erected from the cockroach races the day before.

'And so, the town of Currawong thanks you,' droned Mayor Albright. 'Never before have four children –'

'And a dog,' interrupted April.

'And a dog,' amended the mayor, 'shown such courage. Some might say irrational and ridiculous courage, but courage nonetheless, to apprehend a criminal in our community . . .'

'If she doesn't stop gassing on, I'm just going to go home and watch TV,' muttered April.

'You c-c-can't, this whole event is to honour our b-b-bravery,' said Joe.

'Bravery,' snorted April. 'You dropped Fin on the coach's head. If you'd dropped him half a metre in the other direction, he would be a splat in the middle of some farmer's field right now.'

'. . . and so, in conclusion . . .' prattled the mayor.

'Yay, she's wrapping up,' said Loretta.

'. . . by saving the credibility of the Currawong Cockroach Races you have done a great service to this town. It is my privilege to thank these four young citizens, and their dog, by presenting them with the key to the city,' Mayor Albright concluded.

Everyone applauded. There were cheers and whistles.

Fin smiled. 'We should remember this moment. It's our turning point. The moment we were accepted as part of the Currawong community.'

'Isn't it sweet?' said Loretta, waving at the crowd like the Queen waves at her subjects. 'They've totally forgotten about my cheating in the cockroach races last year. Bless them.'

Mayor Albright reached into her pocket, rifled around for couple of seconds, then pulled out a key and handed it to Joe. The four of them looked at it. It was a regular brass door key.

'That's it?' asked April.

'Isn't a key to a city meant to be . . . well . . . bigger?' asked Fin, looking down at the normal-sized key that lay in Joe's hand.

'Well, Currawong is not a very big town,' said the mayor defensively.

'But this is just an ordinary old key that you found on the ground somewhere, isn't it?' said April, picking it up and glaring at it.

'It's the key to Currawong,' said Mayor Albright.

April snorted. 'No wonder it looks so unimpressive.'

People in the crowd started to boo.

'Put a sock in it,' snapped April. 'You should all be happy. Look in your pockets, you've all got keys to the city too.'

Pumpkin jumped up, snapped the key out of April's hand and swallowed it.

April laughed. 'Good boy.' Even Joe and Fin couldn't stop smiling. Pumpkin panted happily.

The booing grew louder, there was some angry yelling as well.

'Whatever,' said April. 'I'm going home.'

She stalked off. Pumpkin quickly bit the mayor's ankle before chasing after her.

'I guess we're back to square one.' Fin sighed. 'No one likes us again.'

'I think I prefer it this way,' said Joe. 'Popularity is t-t-terrifying.'

'Oh, look, there's Daddy!' exclaimed Loretta, waving to a man wearing surgical scrubs and talking on a mobile phone. 'He must have snuck out of heart surgery to buy me lunch.' She ran over to meet him.

Joe, Fin and April pushed their way through the crowd, which now could be more accurately described as an angry mob, towards the car that was waiting for them. Ingrid had driven them all down to the ceremony. Hopefully, even without Loretta she'd give them a lift home. Dad had stayed in the car because he didn't like crowds or people, plus Constable Pike had yelled at him the day before for leaving the keys in his unregistered helicopter.

The Peski kids slid into the back seat.

'Let's go home,' said Fin.

Dad didn't respond, except to quiver and point at the person sitting in the driver's seat. It was not Ingrid, but it was someone they recognised.

'Professor Maynard!' exclaimed Joe.

'What are you doing here?' asked Fin.

'Responding to reports from the field,' said Professor Maynard.

'What does that mean?' asked Joe.

'Spies,' said Dad.

'Okay, Dad, we've heard enough of your crack-brained theories,' said April.

'No, your father is entirely correct,' said Professor Maynard with a smile. 'You didn't think we'd leave three children with a price on their heads alone and unwatched, did you?'

'You never said there was a price on our heads,' said Fin.

'How much?' asked April curiously.

'You can't kill Fin,' said Joe, guessing the train of his sister's thoughts.

'Why not?' said April. 'I don't need two brothers. Two too many if you ask me.'

'Maybe I'll hand you in,' said Fin, glaring at April.

'Hah,' scoffed April. 'Like to see you try.'

Fin grabbed April in a headlock. April took hold of Fin's arm in a wristlock and wrestling commenced.

'Am I going to have to stun you two with my taser so we can finish this conversation?' asked Professor Maynard.

'Please d-d-do,' said Joe.

'Your caseworkers have reported that you have critically failed in your assignment to assimilate into the local community,' said Professor Maynard sternly, 'and that on the Richtenheimer scale of physically observable morale levels, you displayed a score of only eight-two out of a possible three hundred in personal satisfaction ratings.'

'What does that mean?' asked Fin.

'We have mathematically observed that you are unhappy here,' said Professor Maynard. 'I have graphs and tables on my phone that can prove it. As such, we have set up a new safe house for you. This time in an urban environment, where hopefully you will be better able to acclimatise yourself to the community.'

'What's she saying?' asked April, still trying to give Fin a noogie while everyone else was distracted.

'She's m-m-moving us again,' said Joe.

'No!' protested April. 'I'm not going anywhere.'

'You can't refuse,' said Professor Maynard. 'Setting up a one hundred per cent secure safe house in this day and age of high technology is no easy business. You won't get this chance again. If your identities are compromised here, there's nothing I can do short of arranging for you all to have plastic surgery and move to the Bahamas.'

'Cool,' said Fin. 'I like the beach.'

'I'm not going anywhere,' said April stubbornly. 'I like it here.'

'What?' said Fin. 'Everyone hates you.'

'I don't care,' said April.

'You complain about everything,' said Fin.

'To be fair,' said Joe, 'she complained about everything back in the city too.'

'I like Currawong,' said April. 'It's never boring. Bat-guano crazy, maybe. But never boring.'

'I like it here too,' admitted Joe.

Fin rolled his eyes. 'You just like Loretta.'

Joe blushed.

'Well, she is stunning!' snapped April. 'You'd have to have your eyes gouged out with a melon baller not to notice.'

'I want to stay too,' confessed Fin. 'Everything is very real. Trees, sunshine, cockroach races. It's fun.'

'What about you, Dad?' asked Joe. 'What do you want to do?'

'I don't mind where I am,' said Dad, his voice and his whole body shaking. 'I just want to stay with my kids.' His eyes welled with tears.

In a bout of wildly uncharacteristic empathy, April reached forward and awkwardly put her arm around her dad's shoulders. He hugged her back, his shoulders quivering as he silently wept. It's hard to have a relationship with a father you've only known for a week, especially when he doesn't have a very tight grasp on rationality. But what the children now realised was that although they might not have known their father, he had known them, and he had been missing them for eleven years.

'We'll stay,' said Joe.

'Fine, I suppose,' said Professor Maynard sniffily. 'There is another family in mortal peril, so I suppose they can have the new safe house. But be warned, there is a limit to how well I can protect you in Currawong now. Especially if you make a habit of hijacking hot air balloons.'

Professor Maynard opened the door and swung her leg out.

'Wait!' called Fin. 'Who are our caseworkers? Who have you got watching us?'

'I couldn't possible reveal his or her identity,' said Professor Maynard.

'I bet it's Mr Popov,' said April. 'It isn't normal for a teacher to have an accent and rippling shoulder muscles.'

'No, Joy from the cafe!' said Fin. 'It would explain why she's so miserable. She's a highly trained spy who hates being posted here.'

'Stop guessing! This is not a game!' snapped Professor Maynard, her veneer of affability slipping. 'Don't try to compromise your handlers' cover IDs the same way you've ruined your own.'

Dad glanced out the window and spotted Ingrid sitting on a park bench and waiting for their conversation to end. He opened his mouth to say something but stopped. If he was right, he didn't want to put her in danger.

'If you don't care about your own safety,' said Professor Maynard sternly, 'think about your mother. Think how your actions here can affect her.'

With that mysterious and dramatic statement she got out and slammed the door. A black van pulled up, Professor Maynard climbed in and it sped away.

'I suppose we should be grateful she didn't blow our house up this time,' said Fin. 'She didn't blow it up, did she?'

'I don't think so,' said Dad.

'Come on,' said Joe. 'Let's go home and see.'

Chapter 27

HOME IS WHERE
THE DISASTER IS

As Ingrid drove them home, the Peski kids felt almost like a regular family. As regular as a family with a traumatised father and a mysteriously absent mother could feel. Even Dad had stopped manically fidgeting so much.

'I'm just glad this cockroach craziness is over,' said Fin. 'Now things can go back to normal.'

'They can't go back to normal,' snapped April, 'because nothing here was ever normal to start with.

Everything here is weird and all the people are bonkers.'

'Yeah, but that is normal for Currawong,' said Joe.

'I'm going to have a cup of tea and spend the afternoon separating my daffodil bulbs,' said Dad.

'*Vad är det?!*' cried Ingrid.

They didn't have to speak Swedish to figure out what she was looking at. Up ahead, a huge cloud of black smoke billowed above the trees, directly over their house.

Ingrid floored the accelerator and they flew up the driveway, skidding to a halt on the gravel as they came around the last bend.

'Oh no, oh no, oh no!' wailed Dad.

Their house was on fire. Flames licked out from an upstairs window.

The Peski kids were horror struck.

'This is a nightmare,' murmured Fin.

It was the second time they had seen their home in flames in one week.

'Who would do this to us?' asked Joe.

No one had a clever reply.

Coming soon . . .

THE PESKI KIDS

BEAR IN THE WOODS

ABOUT THE AUTHOR

R. A. Spratt is the author of The Peski Kids, Friday Barnes and The Adventures of Nanny Piggins. In her previous life she was a television writer. Unlike the Peski kids, R. A. Spratt never fights with her brother, but only because he moved to Hong Kong to get away from her. R. A. lives in Bowral, NSW, where she has three chickens, two goldfish and a dog. She also has a husband and two daughters

For more information, visit raspratt.com

HAVE YOU READ FRIDAY BARNES?

HAVE YOU READ NANNY PIGGINS?